12/10/05

Speci ... m
Author to a Precious Sister
Merida with Love.
Stay Blessed!

Mirror in My Heart

by Georgina Happy Crentsil

xulon PRESS

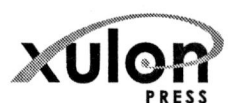

Copyright © 2003 by Georgina Happy Crentsil

Mirror in My Heart
by Georgina Happy Crentsil

Printed in the United States of America

Library of Congress Control Number: 2003091683
ISBN 1-591607-71-X

All rights reserved. No part of this publication may be reproduced or transmitted in any form or by any means without written permission of the publisher.

Unless otherwise indicated, Bible quotations are taken from The Defender's Study Bible, King James Version. Copyright ©1995 by World Publishers, Inc. Grand Rapids, Michigan 49418 USA.

Xulon Press
www.xulonpress.com

To order additional copies, call 1-866-909-BOOK (2665).

CONTENTS

DEDICATIONS vii
ACKNOWLEDGEMENTS ix
INTRODUCTION 11
Chapter One—THE OPEN MINDED WOMAN 13
Chapter Two—THE NARROW MINDED WOMAN 17
Chapter Three—THE SPIRITUAL WOMAN 21
Chapter Four—THE CANAL WOMAN 25
Chapter Five—THE PURPOSEFUL WOMAN 29
Chapter Six—THE AIMLESS WOMAN 33
Chapter Seven—THE GRACEFUL WOMAN 37
Chapter Eight—THE EMBITTERED WOMAN 43
Chapter Nine—THE SECURE WOMAN 47
Chapter Ten—THE INSECURE WOMAN 51
Chapter Eleven—THE FRUITFUL WOMAN 55
Chapter Twelve—THE BARREN WOMAN 61
Chapter Thirteen—THE BEAUTIFUL WOMAN 67
Chapter Fourteen—THE UGLY WOMAN 71
Chapter Fifteen—THE WISE WOMAN 77
Chapter Sixteen—THE FOOLISH WOMAN 83
Chapter Seventeen—THE BLESSED WOMAN 87
Chapter Eighteen—CURSED WOMAN 91
Chapter Nineteen—THE HUMBLE WOMAN 97
Chapter Twenty—THE PROUD WOMAN 101
FINAL WORDS OF ENCOURAGEMENT 105
SPECIAL PRAYER OF DEDICATION 107

GATEWAY TO ABUNDANT LIFE..109
PRAYER FOR SALVATION 111

DEDICATIONS

I dedicate this book to my Dear Husband, **REV. ROBERT CRENTSIL**, whose values; devotion and self-discipline provide unique insight that has helped to mould my character into God's divine pattern

And to our precious children I dedicate this work and pray that the Almighty God will guide them in their choice of spouse according to Prov 31:31:
"Favour is deceitful, and beauty is vain: but a woman that feareth the Lord, she shall be praised" *THIS BOOK IS THEIR LEGACY.*

Above all I dedicate this book to the holy spirit for his love and refining fire in my life. Amen.

ACKNOWLEDGEMENTS

Special thanks to David and Tamara Cordova for
their support and help in making this book a reality.

❦

To God be the glory for entrusting me with this wonderful
gift and the inspiration to express it in writing,

❦

And thank you for giving me the opportunity to
share it with you. Stay blessd!

INTRODUCTION

The Twenty First Century woman is a woman of diverse, intense and deeply challenging experiences which affect the very core of her existence and shape her worldly reality.

Although her experiences are influenced by changes in world trend, the Christian Woman is encouraged to stand out and make a difference. In times of adversity, she is called upon to 'Arise and Shine.' Isaiah 60:1-2. In Mathew 5:13-16, she is described as the salt of the earth and the light of the world, and therefore cannot afford to live her life as if she owned herself, for she" has been bought with a price" and "Ye are not your own" the Bible declares. 1Cor. 6:19-20.

Every Christian Woman faces the unique challenge of being a true reflection of her Master's Nature; a divine privilege which cannot be over looked. Therefore, through these frank revelations of her inner self, she is encouraged to reflect upon her real nature and remove her lamp from under the bushel, (where circumstances may have made her push it) and place it on a lamp stand so she can be a good example to "Glorify her Father who is in Heaven" .Mathew 5:16.

God's Word is a 'lamp unto her feet and a light unto her path.' God's Word is also a mirror that gives her a perfect reflection of her true nature. It helps her take off the mask of hypocrisy and self-deceit, and accept the divine assistance that the Holy Spirit gives, so that she can have a true assessment of herself for progress in her spiritual growth.

Welcome aboard my Dear Sister, on this journey you were destined to take as a Woman. Together we will walk down the alleyways of candidness, through the corridors of life where the transparency of His Word will open doors of insight so that we may end our journey of sober reflections, strengthened upon the solid deck with renewed spiritual Focus!!

MIRROR IN MY HEART will change your life; affect your personal image and self-esteem. So, as you encounter these 'Women of diverse character traits', see if you can recognize yourself in any of these women's lives, and put this " **MIRROR IN YOUR HEART**" to get a true image of yourself for **positive change**.

May God bless and inspire you to greater glory in his wisdom and love as you read this book.

Love,
Rev. Georgina Happy Crentsil

CHAPTER ONE

THE OPEN MINDED WOMAN

The First Woman to be considered is the Open Minded Woman. We will do our best to find out who she is, as we discover some of her qualities and character traits. The Open Minded Woman is so labeled because of her attitude towards life. She is open-minded because she is a woman that is *READY TO MAKE ROOM FOR CHANGE.*

She would not mind adding a little bit more information to what she already has, for she doesn't claim to know it all. She is ready for change because she believes that change is inevitable if one wants to make progress in any area of life, be it Spiritually, Physically, Mentally, Emotionally, Maritally, Materially or Socially.

Political changes affect economic situations and socially accepted behavior in communities, cities and nations, and this in turn has tremendous impact on the financial, social, and sometimes even the physical structures of our families. The effect these changes impose on the Christian Woman, her family and home, causes her to draw upon her inner strength and ability to cope with the day-to-day challenges of her life, while relying upon the strength of the Lord to manifest positive guidelines to structure her responses to these changes and the impact they may have upon her life.

For the Open Minded Woman, responding positively to change comes naturally because she has conquered all normal excuses for compromise, realizing that emotionally and physically, she cannot remain on the same knowledge level and experience her breakthrough.

The Open Minded woman makes an honest assessment of her progress frankly looking at the loop-holes in her character, and being truly repentant of the blunders she may have made, readily accepts the correction and direction God's Word provides.

The Open Minded Woman does not run away from the reflection of her true image. NO! she accepts it, submits herself to reproof and correction and treasures the wisdom that God's Word provides readily making amends where necessary. She accepts her shortcomings and receives correction **without taking offence.**

"Great Peace have those who Love thy Law, and nothing shall offend them." Psalm 119:126.

She makes room for improvement in her life, not foolishly comparing herself to others. The Open Minded Woman does not overlook helpful advice or shake it off as mere criticism to her own hurt and to the disadvantage of the people, her life affects.

As a married woman, she believes in her spouse and willingly works on herself to improve their relationship. She goes out of her way to contribute meaningfully to their relationship to enhance it. In discussions, she avoids arguments, making room for reasoning where necessary.

The open-minded woman takes very careful note of other people's suggestions, because she respects the opinions of others. She does not make conclusions before knowing the facts. She is open minded and level headed because she knows that anyone can make mistakes. She sympathizes with other people's shortcomings and lends a helping hand when needed.

The open-minded woman is very optimistic about the future, for as a career woman; she never stops learning. She looks for opportunities to improve her skills and reflect positively on her field of profession making room for progress where necessary. She believes there is always room for improvement and takes advantage of every well considered opportunity that comes her way ,so she can improve on herself to provide for the continued progress of her family and society.

In communication, she does not rule one out completely because you disagree on a point, but looks for areas of compatibility where the two of you can agree to make room for discussion on those points where conflicting opinions remain.

The open-minded woman is also a God fearing woman who makes an honest assessment of herself in the Light of God's Word. She stands in the mirror of God's Word with all her shortcomings but is not discouraged, because she does not believe in her own ability but agrees with the apostle Paul "I can do all things through Christ who strengthens me".

One major characteristic of the Open Minded Woman is her ability to bring peace wherever there is confusion or misunderstanding because she opens her mouth with wisdom, and her words are full of grace and peace.

As a single woman her open-mindedness gains her respect because of her honest and positive outlook on life and the level of decency and modesty she portrays.

The open minded woman has a very peaceful home or better still, confusion never finds a place to thrive in her home, but evaporates into thin air because she is very honest and fair in her assessment of situations. She **responds positively** to challenging situations instead of **reacting negatively** to them. She controls her responses by evaluating the possible alternatives, choosing the most positive and beneficial one for all concerned. Her husband is a happy man who works hard to improve on himself very much challenged by his wife's unique character and spiritual strength. 1Pet. 3:1-4

She provides her children with the right picture of what life should be by her example, encouragement and good counsel. The Open Minded Woman is a great blessing because there is so much to learn from her as she receives from Christ, her Lord.

She has these virtues as the foundation upon which her character is built; Love, Understanding, Honesty, Kindness and Truth. And with these, she can never fail!

CHAPTER TWO

THE NARROW MINDED WOMAN

The Narrow Minded woman is a very pathetic case, and the direct opposite of the open Minded Woman. If you meet these two in a crowd or congregation you will easily observe their striking differences. We shall attempt in these few pages to reveal some of the features of this unfortunate example of womanhood that saddens the heart of God and grieves the minds of many partners, friends and family members.

Do not forget, she could be a born again Christian woman, but her past and perhaps present experience is that of super spirituality and sheer ignorance. She does not want to invest her God given resources for excellence or to pay the price for acquiring knowledge. She believes she is the final authority on any subject and is ready to argue her position even to the detriment of her important relationships.

The Narrow Minded Woman does not see the need for self-improvement in any area of her life, but believes that what she knows, is all there is to know about life. She is indeed a sad case.

She brags a lot about her achievements not realizing how pathetic her case is in the eyes of her observers. To such a woman, her personal life experiences are the standard with which she judges other people. And believe me, in her mind she always comes out on top with very unfair results for others. In fact, trying to correct this type of woman will surely put you on her list of enemies, who she thinks are envious or jealous of her achievements. She concludes you do not appreciate her enough if you do not shower her with flattering words or praises, in spite of the numerous character flaws you may have observed about her.

The truth is, she does not appreciate change if it will affect her mindset of what she thinks should be. Though she may be religious, the narrow-minded woman sees the cross as a threat to her independence. She is very self-indulgent and blames others for the results of her own careless mistakes, never taking responsibility for her actions. She is so cunning in her nature that she can twist any argument, to the point where she is completely right even if she was wrong.

To experience positive change, the narrow minded woman will have to open up herself completely to the deep inner workings of God's Holy Spirit, and cry out with the Psalmist "Open thou my eyes that I may behold wondrous Things out of thy law" Ps. 119:18.

The narrow-minded woman has to broaden her horizon, and realize that there is more to life than what she knows. She has to stop blaming all her misfortunes on others and step out of the mediocre mentality she has so much confined herself, thus placing a limitation on her progress in the life God has planned for her. Are you a narrow-minded woman?. Or do you know of one?. Well, lets take counsel from God's word, it has the solution to the problems in every life situation.

First of all, the narrow-minded woman needs to discover her plight, acknowledge the deformity in her image and honestly and humble seek help from the word of God and from good counselors. She must be ready to pay the price of abandoning her pride to acquire knowledge because the narrow-mindedness she has maintained has made her arrogant and ignorant. The Bible describes her in 2Tim. 3:7, as "Ever learning and never able to come to the knowledge of the truth." She needs to be settled under one good spiritual authority or local assembly for systematic spiritual nourishment instead of moving from one Church membership to the other because of offence and lack of spiritual submission. She has to desire "the sincere milk of God's Word, so she can grow thereby", (1Peter. 2:2) and also take the admonishing in Hebrew 6:1-3, where the Bible instructs her to grow unto maturity leaving behind the elementary principles of the doctrine of Christ.

She needs to give heed to Hebrews 5:12~14, which encourages her to feed on the strong meat of Gods Word, so that her spiritual senses can be exercised for a deeper walk of faith. This will enable her to walk in Spiritual discernment and make her a great source of help and inspiration unto many. All she needs to do is to accept guidance and open up to good counsel that will result in Fruitfulness in her Christian life to the Glory of God. And with this change of attitude and mindset, she will become a ready vessel, able to achieve great victories in Gods Kingdom.

The Bible encourages us to "grow in grace and in the knowledge of our Lord and Savior Jesus Christ". For the narrow-minded woman this verse gives her the opportunity to step out of her defeated Christian life, into an abundant life of Peace, Joy and Blessings. Her fulfillment and joy in life will be very much determined by how ready she is for change and the positive impact she can make on the lives of the people she interacts with. What she needs is a complete change of attitude from her narrow-mindedness to open-mindedness. And, through the grace of our Lord Jesus Christ, she will become a vessel of Honour, prepared for her Master's use and Destined to bring Him Glory and Praise! Amen!!!

CHAPTER THREE

THE SPIRITUAL WOMAN

The Spiritual Woman is a spirit filled woman, whose foundation is firmly rooted in the Word of God. Her spiritual attitude is best described by Jesus' Words in Matt: 5:6 " Blessed are those who hunger and thirst after righteousness, for they shall be filled."

Truly she never seems to have enough of God, but like David of old, she cries out

"Oh God, thou art my God, early will I seek thee, my soul thirsteth for thee, my flesh longeth for thee in a dry and thirsty land where no water is". Ps. 63:1-2.

Her heart continually longs for deep intimacy with her God, vibrating with the strong passion and desire for more of Him. Realization that "Deep Calleth Unto the Deep," her hungry soul relentlessly awaits the sound of His water spouts! And surely she shall be filled to overflowing with His Devine Love, and blessed with His sweet and refreshing Presence. For his word declares," if you seek me you shall find me when you search for me with all your heart!!!"

She is a woman with rich spiritual experiences who places priority on enhancing her relationship with her Lord. Carnality and compromise have no place in her life, for she is dead to self and alive unto God.

Her unique characteristic is her total submission to the Holy Spirit. To her, **worshiping God in spirit and in truth is a life long pursuit**, for she has no time to meddle in the unfruitful works of darkness. The desire of her heart is to please God, and because of her deep devotion and relentless effort for Spiritual excellence, God is not ashamed to be called her Father.

Some of the Spiritual Woman's life experiences can be likened to the fruit bearing branch in God's Vineyard, John 15:1-8. For He may sometimes **"set her up"** for special times of **testing** or **pruning** with the divine purpose of promoting her to greater heights of spiritual achievement and fruitfulness. God is very confident of her loyalty to Him. He knows he can trust her, for in the time of adversity, she declares with the Psalmist, **"My heart is fixed, oh God, my heart is fixed, I will sing and give praise. (Ps. 57:7).**

The secret to her exceptional quality of strength is her total dependence on God, for **Love, guidance** and **protection.** She is filled with God's divine grace and power, thus making her quiet a challenge to keep pace with spiritually. Her spiritual wells never seem to dry up but are always vibrant with divine life, for her life-giving source is God Himself. The Holy Spirit, her divine companion, is so real in her life, you can see Him through the clear manifestation of His fruits demonstrated through her character, and some of these fruits which are worth mentioning are; **Love, Faith, Joy, Humility, Forgiveness, Patience, Goodness, Temperance, Gentleness and Self-control.** She is a vessel of honor, ready and meet for her Master's use, for she bears her fruit in season and out of season.

Looking at the unique qualities of the spiritual woman, you may see her example as too good to be true or get discouraged in your efforts to follow in her foot steps, and maybe give up on yourself completely, seeing her spiritual standard as too high or far fetched. But I have news for you, for although the spiritual woman is a woman of faith and virtue, and a woman whose relationship with

God is based on the Word of God, like Paul, she does not boast of her own righteousness, but **the righteousness which God imputes upon her by his divine act of grace and mercy through her personal faith in Jesus Christ.**

She takes her walk of faith with God a step at a time. Her first step is in **Psalm 51; a place of genuine repentance**, "Have mercy upon me O God, according to thy lovingkindness: according unto the multitude of thy tender mercies blot out my transgressions." she then moves on to **Lamentations 3:22-27** where she depends only on **God's mercy, forgiveness and acceptance**, "It is of the Lord's mercies that we are not consumed, because His compassions fail not..." She also knows that "For by grace are ye saved through faith; and that not of yourselves: it is the gift of God: Not of works, lest any man should boast. Ephesians 2:8-9. If you can sincerely and soberly trace her steps, you will discover how humble and meek she is. She is not superficial or super spiritual in her attitude, but is very sober and sincere in her assessment of herself.

It is good to take note of the fact that she did not become such an exceptional character overnight but started from right where you may find yourself now; a place of total unworthiness, in need of God's grace and strength. But she has learned the secret of trusting in the Devine Hand of God, walking daily in obedience and submission to His Word.

To help you know and understand the background to her wonderful spiritual progress, you would do well to study the lives of some of her biblical counter parts like; Rahab the harlot Joshua 2:1-24 ,Heb.11:31., Ruth the Moabite, Ruth 2:4-14; 4:13-22. Mary of Bethany, John 11:2; 12:1-8, Hannah the mother of Samuel,1Samuel 1and2; Zippora the wife of Moses, Exodus 4:24-26; the Shunnamite Woman,2 Kings 4: 8-37; the Canaanite woman from Tyre and Sidon, Mathew 15:21-28 and Mary Magdalene, the first woman Evangelist after the Resurrection. Mark 16:9-11; John 20:1-18. All these were women who did not allow their past or present circumstances to hinder their personal faith in God, nor did they allow anything, including bitter disappointment to deter them from the purpose and Destiny that God's Word alone had set before them.

Indeed they are described as spiritual because it took more than human strength and ability to walk with God the way they did. I encourage you to study their life experiences and follow their good examples of self-denial, undaunted faith and undiluted devotion to God, and your life will never be the same again, but will bring Glory to God and Blessing to mankind. You will become a vessel of honor in word and in deed. Above all, you will become a firebrand in the hand of God and a threat to the enemy as long as you hook up to the fuel source of prayer, faith and obedience to God's Word.

Arise! Pursue spiritual excellence and leave a positive mark on your generation. Welcome to the wonderful world of the spiritual woman.

You will love it! Bon voyage!

CHAPTER FOUR

THE CARNAL WOMAN

The woman we are about to consider is the most unfortunate character you can come across in any Christian group or home. Although she is born again, like Esau she does not see the importance of her spiritual birthright nor does she place priority on the things that will add to her Christian character. She can be very active in religious activities and yet build a shield of passive acceptance, which she uses as a self-defense against any Word of God that seeks to expose her carnal desires or attitudes.

She is a woman that is controlled by her five senses because she is not ready to pay the costly price of self-denial for the **"Excellency of the knowledge of Christ Jesus her Lord" Phil. 3:8** .She sees Christianity as an easy escape from the problems of life and a means of finding tolerance and acceptance among other Christians. You might say she is using her association with Christians as a means of gaining respectability in her social group, but when it comes to living according to what God's Word says, she tends to alter her 'Christian stand' using worldly trends and behavioral acceptances as justification to compromise; all in pursuit of satisfying her carnal desires.

You can easily identify her because, though she looks very spiritual on the outside; a closer look reveals all her carnal traits such as **un-forgiveness, bitterness, slander, boasting and self-gratification**. Worshipping God in spirit and in truth does not appeal to her at all because even though she is a Christian, she still longs for the delicacies of Egypt like Israel did in the wilderness. Her carnal desires hinder her from experiencing a divine encounter with the Lord; therefore her Christian life is a dry and fruitless one. She cannot please God because she is in the flesh from the moment she awakens to the silencing of her mind in sleep, never acknowledging Him who gave her breath to live another day. Rom. 8:8.

The truth is, Personal Devotional life, Bible study, Fasting and Prayer are not part of her Christian vocabulary. She is spiritually fruitless and barren because she has refused the pruning knife of the Vinedresser, **John 15:1**. She forgets that her Lord desires her to bring forth **more fruit** unto His glory. She does not make any real effort to know Jesus Christ intimately. She is still in **the shallow waters of commitment** deciding how much of a relationship with Jesus she can 'live with.' To her, 'launching out into the deep waters of trust in Gods Word and direction for her life' is not very important with respect to her Christian experience. In her opinion, this is not too necessary or even desirable. She would rather remain in her comfort zone of compromise and shameful defeat in her spiritual walk with God. She has lost sight of the fact that a day of reckoning awaits her and that she will have to give an account of what she did with her life as a child of God.

Unfortunately, as she persists in her carnal lifestyle, she continues to lose her passion for the salvation of souls and never sees the importance, and like the seed, which fell among thorns in Jesus parable of the sower, **she cannot bear abiding fruits for her Lord. Matt.13: 7-22.** She has lost her first love, **Jesus Christ**, as He stands at the door of her heart knocking and waiting for an opportunity to **renew an intimate relationship** with her. {Rev.3:20}

Until she dies to 'self' and live unto God she can never experience increase and progress in her Christian life.

For the carnal woman, the admonishing of Christ to take up her cross and follow Him on a daily basis is the pathway to her recovery.

In **Col. 3:1** Paul says" if she is risen with Christ, then her affection and desire must be centered on Christ above and not on the things of this earth"{paraphrased}, because friendship with the world is enmity with God, **James 4:4** and ye cannot serve two masters, you will either hate one or love the other, the bible declares. **Matt. 6:24.**

Lukewarmness is the major characteristic of the **carnal woman**, which puts her in grave danger because Christ warns He will spew her out of is His Mouth. (Rev. 3:15 & 16). Returning to her first love in true repentance and acknowledgement of her backslidden state is the first step to recovery, while pursuing a life of total dependence on the Word of God will yield untold results in her life for God's Glory.

Her breakthrough will come when she can genuinely cry out as John the Baptist did, **"He must increase and I must decrease"**. Until the 'I' which is the **"Self"** in her life is dethroned, Jesus will never occupy His rightful place on the throne of her heart, and therefore cannot be revealed through her life in fruitful Service. The only way to break this hold of carnality in her life is to **lift Jesus up** so '**He can draw all men unto Himself**.' According to **Matt. 5:6,** the solution to her Spiritual bankruptcy is to **Hunger** and **Thirst** after **Righteousness** for then and only then can she be **Filled**. For out of her belly the Living Waters will flow to quench her own thirst and that of the needy around her so that **through her renewed selfless character and good example of true Christianity, her life will bear abiding fruits to the Glory of God.**

CHAPTER FIVE

THE PURPOSEFUL WOMAN

I t is a great joy to discuss this wonderful character for she brings joy to the Heart of God, and satisfaction to societies and families everywhere. For where ever the Purposeful Woman is, there is UNITY OF PURPOSE, INCREASE, PRODUCTIVITY AND, PROSPERITY!

The characteristics of the purposeful woman are so unique that it is a privilege to know her and walk with her on life's journey.

She is a Woman of Vision and Foresight. These distinct life saving ingredients in her character are there to be a help to all those she comes in contact with because, **'Where there is no Vision the people perish'** {THAT IS, THEY LIVE AIMLESSLY AND WALK CARELESSLY}. She knows her worth and understands the reason why she is on earth, therefore instead of being discouraged by the daily challenges that come her way, she allows herself to be inspired by them so that she can move on to a life of Excellence. **She believes that God, her Creator, has the blueprint for her life, and therefore she can depend on the Holy Spirit for insight and guidance in every Decision that she makes.** Knowing God's

Agenda and plan for her life is her greatest desire, and her goal and aim is to fulfill it.

The purposeful woman sees God as a God of objectivity and plan, a God of purpose who does everything according to His own predetermined counsel. Therefore she depends on His counsel and strength to carry on in pursuit of her life goals. **She is a determined woman who sees impediments and challenges as opportunities and stepping-stones to reach unto greater heights of excellence. In the face of challenges she always has this chorus to sing; "I'm going on I'm going on, I'm going on towards the Mark, towards my Goal! So many lives depend on what I do, give me the Strength, Dear Lord, I'm going on for you".** Her life stands on the foundation of a deep intimate relationship with her Lord. She is a woman of Destiny, selfless and ready to pay the price necessary to see her dreams fulfilled within the scope of Gods Plan for her life. **She believes that her breakthrough in life does not affect herself only, but that many people's Destinies are linked to hers. With this sense of responsibility, the purposeful woman faces every challenge with renewed strength and determination from the Lord.**

She doesn't move on impulse or dive into activity on the spur of the moment, just because she conceives an idea, but waits on the Lord, and with good counsel from the right sources, draws a plan of action or adapts the right strategy that will help bring her Vision to pass. She therefore responds to situations as a woman of knowledge and insight, and very resolute in decision-making. She hates procrastination and indecision because she knows what she wants and goes for it. **She has a standard set for life, based on balanced principles, and will never settle for anything below her determined goal.** She avoids compromise and anything that will make her lose focus. She is determined to reach her goal at all cost and ready to defend what she believes in using the Right Standing of Gods Word and Authority.

One very notable characteristic of the purposeful woman is that she is not afraid to make mistakes. She is a risk taker but she is not foolish. She does not rush headlong into any situation or resume any project without first taking a moment to analyze it or count the cost.

She believes that to make progress in life, she must be bold to take initiatives to fulfill the need with out fear of failure, but ready to learn from her mistakes. She is very honest with her own personal conduct and takes time out every now and then to take stock and assess her own performance, thus making room for improvement and pursuing her God given goals with Purpose and determination.

In her relationships the Purposeful Woman focuses more on how she can improve on herself for better results. She takes correction and counsel without offense because she believes **there is always something new to learn, or perhaps to let go of, if one wants to be 'friendship material".**

She is indeed a blessing to be with, because her attitude towards life is so positive and down to earth. She makes life look so simple and easy you would think she could easily reach out to the moon, grasp it and pull it down. She is confident and bold without pretense, false modesty or the need for public recognition.

The purposeful woman believes in taking decisive steps in life but hates procrastination. It is not her life style to abandon any project with flimsy excuses, because she counts the cost and prepares adequately before she begins. Get this woman of purpose on any project of yours and you are bound to succeed because of her relentless zeal and purposeful steps.

God help our families and Churches to produce more Purposeful Women, for the world needs them to face the unpredictable challenges ahead. Our children need purposeful mothers to give them guidance and good balance for their future. And there is a great need in society and families for such purposeful women to bring many way ward husbands back on track, through their patience, wise counsel, undaunted faith and firm focus.

To her, giving up in the face of challenges is a sign of betrayal and disloyalty to her God, to society, her family and herself. Therefore she is always ready to pay the price for her God given Visions and Dreams to be fulfilled.

If you want the Purposeful Woman for a wife, then you should be a man of Strength and Vision. In other words, the Purposeful Woman has the potential of making an aimless man,

a man of Vision and Purpose who is ready to scale any mountain and move every obstacle, till he sees his dreams fulfilled. She has a way of provoking you unto good works by her wise counsel and encouragement. When she is around, there will always be a way out of any difficult situation. She is a woman of great achievement, and the secret to her boldness and courage is her total dependence on God for guidance and strength.

In conclusion, the purposeful woman's success story makes her a blessing unto many because, through her rich store of experiences, she is able to motivate others into achieving their own God given dreams and goals.

She has a way of encouraging and motivating a self defeated visionary to resume and complete an abandoned project, always ready to sacrifice her resources and time to help such individuals fulfill their God given Dreams.

She specializes in bringing peace into broken relationships, by giving the parties involved a renewed vision to unite for peace and progress. They could be a troubled couple facing challenges in their relationship, or problems between business partners or members of a church family. On every front, she is a genius in peace making because she believes and practices; *"UNITY OF SPIRIT AND PURPOSE FOR PRODUCTIVITY IN GOD'S KINGDOM".*

Indeed the Purposeful Woman adds to Life and to Society. She is a Fulfilled Woman!!!

CHAPTER SIX

THE AIMLESS WOMAN

The Aimless Woman is a woman who has lost track of the path of righteousness and forsaken the guide of her youth, the HOLY SPIRIT. She knows of her heritage as a child of God but has lost the ability to claim her rightful inheritance as a Christian.

She is like a ship at sea without a captain or sailor. She has no **"assurance of her salvation,"** but is easily blown to and fro by any new idea or doctrine. She knows that **"those that are led by the Spirit of God are the sons of God,"** but the price of following the Holy Spirit closely is too high for her to pay, as it requires commitment. Oh she wishes she could also exhibit some of the qualities of the Purposeful Woman, but that is how far she gets, **"wishful thinking"**, nothing more. Forsaking the ancient landmarks of God's Word, she trudges on aimlessly along life's highway reacting to trouble and difficult situations in her own strength, never knowing her Father's Love and Guiding Hand.

Oh what a waste! Unless she quickly recovers her wasted years of idleness and applies a good dose of self-discipline, total repentance and renewed commitment to Gods Word and Plan for her life, she is set on the road to destruction where aimless people of confused identities and procrastinating spirits end.

Her closest companion is ignorance. She lacks knowledge and information of God's purpose for her life and for this reason she has no personal agenda in life, no real responsibility, "Anything goes" is her motto, and it is evident in her conduct, appearance, work and home. Because she has not discovered her God given potential in life, she does not bless anyone. Yet it is interesting to note that when she is positively influenced, the Aimless Woman can portray glimpses of untapped resources of talents and abilities that are lying dormant underneath the covering of ignorance, due to laziness and lack of proper focus.

Truly she achieves nothing, but is a busy body given to much idleness. She often gets into trouble because she is a meddler and tattler, very rash with her tongue spewing out her ignorance for all to see.

Oh for this woman, the Holy Spirit waits patiently "until the day dawns and the day star arises in her heart" to give her direction. Her change will come when she humbly accepts her state of ignorance, and opens up completely for good counsel. By laying a hold on purpose and receiving the knowledge of her God given agenda in life, she will be able to recover every lost ground and receive restoration for her wasted years. All she needs is a good dose of faith, hope, hard work and self discipline. The Aimless Woman may admire or worse still criticize the achievements of the Purposeful Woman. But her own lack of achievement is the result of her fruitless labor of chasing after the wind of idleness never settling down to any meaningful project or focusing in any positive direction and sticking to it faithfully unto completion. She is plagued with diseases like LAZINESS, LOVE OF LEISURE, ENVY, BITTERNESS, JEALOUSY, and HATRED. Thus, she has paralyzed her God given potential, which lies underneath a mountain of lazy and flimsy excuses, which other Women of Purpose have willingly overcome with the help and grace of God.

For the aimless woman, James has a word of advise in James 1:5 "If any of you lack wisdom, let him ask of God which giveth to all men liberally and upbraideth not, and it shall be given him." All she has to do is ask God for Wisdom, so she can receive direction for her life. The Bible says, "Where there is no vision the people walk aimlessly and live carelessly." A woman who has Vision is a woman with direction and purpose because Vision will give strength to Purpose, which will motivate and strengthen one to press on even in the face of challenges, for where there's vision and purpose there is hope and God's Word declares, "And hope maketh not ashamed." Rom. 5:5

The Bible says about Jesus... "For the joy that was set before him, he endured the cross, despising the shame and is set down at the right hand of the Majesty of God." Heb. 12:2

Jesus' vision for redeeming man would never have been accomplished if he had not looked steadfastly towards the Purpose he was going to achieve after his death and resurrection.

The Aimless Woman's lack of motivation can be due to the fact that she may be completely ignorant of her purpose in life or does not see the importance of pursuing any life goal. This attitude towards life has made the Aimless Woman an ineffective tool in God's house.

Her best example in the bible is that of the Five Foolish Virgins who took their burning lamps to meet the Bridegroom, but failed to take extra oil for any possible delay. They were virgins all right, they also had burning lamps but they lacked the foresight and adequate preparation that goes with the unique privilege of meeting the Bridegroom, thus they were left behind. Matt.25:1-14..

Looking into the body of Christ today, many such women trudge in and out of Churches and religious meetings with no purpose, focus or enlightenment so far as God's agenda for their personal lives are concerned.

Society is filled with a lot of women with immense potential who are wasting away due to lack of proper focus and personal motivation in life. The fact is if a lot more women would discover their God given potential and not necessarily be in competition with anyone, but rather direct their energies into worth while and fruitful ventures, the world will be a better place to live in. Our children will have better role models in Mothers, Aunties, Sisters, and Grandmothers. And our Churches will open more day cares, schools, rehabilitation centers and projects that can benefit the society they live in while building the kingdom of God.

The world is waiting for the day when Women of Purpose will arise in Unity to accomplish one goal, that is, to give purpose and direction to our younger generation, a generation under tremendous attack from the negative effects of increased technology and moral decadence. This can happen only when the Aimless Woman discovers her personal potential and purpose in life, so she can positively influence her Family and Society. God waits patiently to lend a helping hand through the power of the Holy Spirit. For He alone can transform our human weakness into divine capability, that can change an Aimless Woman into a Purposeful one.

CHAPTER SEVEN

THE GRACEFUL WOMAN

The Graceful Woman is a character filled with immense treasure and blessings. She is a close acquaintance of the embittered woman, but very different in all aspects. Their closeness can be traced to the fact that life seems to have dealt with them in similar ways. These two women have all gone through the difficult challenges of life, such as disappointment, ingratitude from people they have helped, the painful experience of betrayal, rejection from friends or relations who do not benefit from their generosity any more, due to unfortunate life circumstance like loss of position or wealth which may be due to ill health, divorce or loss of a good social status.

This painful realization has brought these two women to a major crossroads in life, where they need to make decision to either stay on top of their circumstances or decline in self pity, revenge, regret and painful despair. And here, at this crossroads comes the striking difference between these two women. Whereas her precious sister "embittered" goes down the pathway of self-destruction and pride, the graceful woman looks "unto Jesus the author and finisher of her faith". She remembers God's word, which says, "**When thou passest through the waters, I will be with thee; and through the rivers, they shall not overflow thee: when thou walkest through the fire, thou shalt not be burned; neither shall the flame kindle upon thee." Isaiah 43:2.**

The graceful woman believes that no matter what disappointment or injustice she may experience at the hands of man, her relationship with God is the bedrock upon which her life stands. She does not allow the wrongs that people may have done to her create bitterness in her soul. She is careful to remember God's words to **"Keep thy heart with all diligence for out of it are the issues of life." Prov.4:23 and,** that **"If I regard iniquity in my heart the Lord will not hear me." Ps.66:18.** She is not vengeful. The graceful woman is a woman who knows God and understands that the painful experiences and challenges she's gone through in life are the very tools that have been used by God to bring out the refined character in her that makes her so unique. (2Cor. 1:3-5) She harbors no grievances, has no bitterness and blames no one for her pitfalls in life.

The graceful woman has learned that in her time of shame or disappointment, God is her strength and shield. She knows that her God cannot fail her. For He will surely show up at the right time to be the lifter up of her head. She has learned how to draw upon the help and comfort of the Holy Spirit. As a result, she is always full of the life and sweetness of God's Divine Grace. She has learned the secret of walking with God in *'COVENANT RELATIONSHIP'* where the only thing that matters is whether she is walking and living a life pleasing unto Him or not. She knows that in spite of all the circumstances that may confront or challenge her in life, at the end of the day it is what God says about the situation that matters or makes the difference.

She knows that the bible says; "For there is hope of a tree, if it be cut down, that it will sprout again, and that the tender branch will not cease." (Job 14:7) The graceful woman's divine link with God makes her a refreshing source of encouragement when one is down and out. She is "like a tree planted by the rivers of waters she bears her fruits in season and out of season. She cannot be a disappointment to God. The graceful woman is a spiritual woman who understands Gods divine timings and seasons in the lives of His covenant people. She knows that her destiny is in God's hands and this realization creates a deep sense of peaceful assurance in her heart that manifest itself in the graceful manner in which she carries herself in spite of her adverse circumstances.

Oh I wish I could say that such inner beauty and peace was brought about by peaceful and favorable circumstances. But on the contrary, though the graceful woman has had her share of life's challenges, she has learned how to cast her cares on the Lord, allowing His Word to deal with her own rebellions and the insecurities within her heart so that in the midst of the storm, she stands strong with her feet firmly rooted in the Word of God which is her anchor.

She is full of forgiveness and compassion. She is so sure of 'an expected end from God' (Jer:29: 11) that she has no room for pity parties and self-destructive thoughts. Her life's balance can be traced to such unique qualities like love, forgiveness, kindness, patience, gentleness, faith, hope and self-control.

Her ability to pick herself up after a difficult experience, learn the lessons she has to learn, forget the discouragement of the past and still forge her way through life with faith lifted high, makes the graceful woman a unique and rewarding contribution to God's purpose in creating women. She is a blessing and an inspiration to womanhood. She is the one God was referring to as a "helper suitable for man." Her example and counter part in the bible is Abigail the wife of Nabal "fool".

In her bitter experience of being married to Nabal (a man who had no fear of God) she was still able to maintain her gracefulness and rich character. Abigail was a woman who was full of God's wisdom. She gathered information about David, and was abreast with what God was doing in Israel. That combined with her sweet 'spirit and character' produced in her a divine sense of responsibility which resulted in a fast, calculated action producing a refined and seasoned speech to David which was an intervention so divine that it prevented David from taking vengeance into his own hands by destroying her household including her ungrateful husband and herself. In the end David the anointed servant of God could not resist such inner qualities of grace combined with her sweet beauty; he ended up marrying her after God had struck Nabal (her foolish husband) dead.

Oh, there are many such potential situations out there which could have a happy ending like Abigail's if only such women would allow the Holy Spirit to have his full access into their lives and to give Jesus His rightful place in their hearts, in the midst of their challenging circumstances. The graceful woman is one who does not allow her potentials in life to die with bitter experiences and disappointment, she believes that "the righteous falls seven time and rises up again." She also believes that out of her 'crucified circumstance,' will come her "Resurrection Morning" for she declares on her dark and gloomy days, "weeping may endure for a night but joy cometh in the morning." Ps.30:5.

The graceful woman is a woman that is full of hope. She knows how to believe God for the impossible. She is like Abraham who against hope, believed in hope. She believes in "the God which calleth those things which be not as though they were." Romans 4:17-20

In short, the graceful woman has risen out of a state of hopelessness and great disappoints into a place of glorious liberty and freedom from all cares and fretful anxieties. She is so peaceful and stable you could almost wonder if she has ever known adversity. If she is an unmarried woman she is free of anxiety and fear of growing old. She believes in living her life to the fullest in the light of God's predetermined counsel concerning her. Instead of worrying about the things, which are not, she focuses on the opportunities given her by God, and gives her fullest attention to the things that will make her life more meaningful to herself and a blessing to God and to men.

She is confident that in God's own time her change will come and her 'Mr. Right' will show-up as she faithfully walks with God. She has no set backs because she refuses to acknowledge them as such. She rather uses seeming set backs as propelling tools and instruments for progress in her life. As a married woman, a challenge in marriage is always an opportunity to learn something new and depend on God for a way of escape from whatever destructive purpose the enemy may have up his sleeves.

Do not forget that the Graceful Woman may have been taken advantage of. She may have seen betrayal from friends and loved ones. She may have experienced heartbreaks on many levels, but the graceful woman is a woman who lives on top of her experiences in life, be it good or bad. She has learned the secret of the Psalmist when he says: "Whom have I in heaven but Thee? And there is none upon earth that I desire beside Thee." (Ps.73:25)

She has made God and her relationship with Him her focus. No wonder her heart is full of forgiveness, love and compassion even for those who have hurt her. She is constantly praying that God will forgive them and give them the opportunity to know Him as she does. Her gracefulness and charm is like a jewel in the hand of God, which He proudly displays to attract the wayward and lost unto Himself. Like the spiritual woman, she is dead to self and alive unto God, for she cries out "**He** must increase and **I** must decrease." That is her secret. She knows the blessings of being forgiven her sins by God, and so she has learned the secret that forgiving her fellowman is a sign of appreciation and obedience to God. She is Beautiful!

CHAPTER EIGHT

THE EMBITTERED WOMAN

The woman we are about to discuss is a character that needs to be handled with care and great concern. She is a very unfortunate woman because no one seems to understand her or her grievance. Her life seems to constantly spew out such unpleasantness that she is a constant embarrassment even to herself and to those who love her.

The unfortunate thing about her situation is the fact that circumstances have given her the wrong conclusion about herself because she believes that nobody loves or really cares about her. She has sadly concluded that God has also forgotten her. Her past experiences of disappointment and lack of appreciation for certain sacrifices she made for others in life has left a deep bitter feeling, that only the tender and far reaching hand of the HOLY SPIRIT can Heal. He is the divine Comforter and He alone has the power to break the chain of unforgiveness, regret, shame and pain that has locked this precious child of God in the gall of bitterness.

In fact, the notable thing one needs to know about the embittered woman is the feeling that not only has her generosity been abused, but she feels very much cheated in life. You need to know that the embittered woman used to be a very sweet young lady ready to sacrifice to bring joy to the people she loved, for whom she was ready to give of her most treasured possessions such as; **Time, Affection and Wealth.**

It is of great importance that we throw a little light on some of the unique characteristics of the Embittered Woman which made her vulnerable and susceptible to the pain and heartache she experienced in life;

The embittered woman is one who had been taken advantage of because of her naivety and softness of heart. She had given so much of herself with such unreservedness that was almost equal to martyrdom for the people she loved. But now, she has been awakened by the circumstances of disappointment, pain and rejection, as if out of a deep sleep, with the painful realization of being used and spent. This has resulted in the painful feeling of being unappreciated, neglected and ignored. In retaliation, the embittered woman reacts to her deep-seated feelings with out bursts of anger and rage at the slightest expression of resistance or an opposing opinion from anyone. Unfortunately for her, this one time sweet lady sometimes flares up in front of strangers who leave her presence with a very bad impression of her character, not knowing what injustices she may have suffered in life. And that realization even angers and hurts her the more, knowing that her image has been tarnished in the eyes of people she looked up to for sympathy and respect. This woman is a very lonely and sad woman. To her, life has been very unfair.

If this woman is a Christian woman, (which is very possible) she is very loud and vengeful in praying judgmental prayers against people who have offended or disappointed her. No matter how excited or happy she may be at a particular time, the slightest occurrence, or reference to any of her past painful and unfortunate experiences, always awakens the sickening feeling of pain in the very pit of her stomach and that marks the end of her joy.

Thus, she waits and hopes secretly and desperately for the day when God will inflict a greater measure of pain on all those who have hurt or offended her in life. She has become so bitter; she has lost every trace of mercy or forgiveness in her bowels. She may temporarily seem to have forgiven someone, but the truth is she has not. Looking at the extent of her hurts she feels justified in wishing evil for those who have offended her and counts them as enemies and even looks out for sympathizer to agree with her by drawing attention to the extent of pain they may have caused her.

Some of the people who fall into the category of her enemies may be a husband, a relative, a friend, a neighbor, a co-worker or even her own child, since all of these persons in one way or the other may have contributed to her present embittered condition. If her pain or disappointment had to do with an unsuccessful relationship with a man, she tends to build an invisible shield of self-defense around herself, by putting up a disdainful attitude towards men in general, thus shutting out the possibility of any meaningful relationship, for fear of being hurt again.

It is unfortunate that these painful memories seem unbearable to her, but they continue to be this way because she has not given them to God who alone can help her experience true forgiveness in her heart, so she can receive the Joy of His Spiritual Love and the Peace of His Devine Comfort.

If the embittered woman is single her attitude or behavior reveals a strong foundation of lack of trust in men, thus turning away many potentially good suitors, because the very air of rebuff around her puts them off. She is so strongly bound to the hurts of her past that she has lost grip on all the possible joys for her future.

What a pity! This woman needs help! But unfortunately even within the Christian Community, such hurting women are misunderstood because of their distorted characters. They are ignored as "difficult cases" that only 'spiritual giants' can handle. But the truth is; it will take an understanding attitude, a gentle touch, a listening ear, a loving look and a tender word of encouragement from an Open Minded and Spiritual Woman, filled with God's love and a great level of humility to help restore joy and peace into the life of this Precious but erring Child of God.

For the embittered woman I have these final words of encouragement. It is not over yet! All you need to do is wake up from the sleep of hopeless abandonment of your God given dreams and qualities and confess the bitterness and un-forgiveness in your heart to God.

Precious Child of God, allow the Love of God to refresh your soul. Open your heart to the gentle healing touch of the Holy Spirit and receive Grace from God to forgive and release all those who have offended and despitefully used you in the past. This is the fastest way to healing and recovery. And don't forget that God is a God of divine restoration who is able to restore to you; 'the years that the locust, the caterpillar, the canker worm and the palmer worm has eaten.' Your wasted years shall be restored to you bountifully. .And He is able to give you double for your Trouble! Your example of God's Promised Restoration is found in the life of Job. After he had forgiven and prayed for his ungrateful friends who accused him of sin in the time of his calamity, he was **completely restored a double portion** of all that he had lost. He received double for his Trouble, and so will you!

The wilderness in your life will become a fruitful field, if you can agree with the psalmist and declare, "...many there be which say of my Soul, there is no help for him in God. Selah. But thou, Oh Lord, art a shield for me; my glory, and the lifter up of my head. "Ps.3:2-3.

Declare with the psalmist; "Show me a token for good; that they which hate me may see it, and be ashamed: because thou, Lord, hast holpen me, and comforted me."Ps.86:17.

Link up your life to the Holy Spirit and receive His love and comfort by shaking off every garment of heaviness and pain and replace it with an attitude of thankfulness, gratitude and praise unto God! May the Lord help you as you make all the effort to receive His unfailing, and unchanging Grace. Keep Smiling. God Loves You! This is the beginning of a new life of Joy and Peace. Bravo!!! STAY BLESSED!!!

CHAPTER NINE

THE SECURE WOMAN

The secure woman is a character of great demand in our society and world today. The New Millennium has produced unexpected changes and happenings that demand a great level of balance and strong sense of security for any woman who will be able to make it, for her own self, her family and the society she lives in.

The secure woman is a woman of immense strength and great balance. And for that matter, she is a woman of great achievements. There are many things that make a woman feel secure in life. Things like a loving and faithful husband, a good and rewarding profession, status in society, financial or material wealth, a good upbringing from a family environment of Love where there is a great sense of belonging, all these contribute to a feeling of security. These are all very important factors that may add up to make a woman feel secure in one way or the other. But, the secure woman we want to discuss is one whose security does not end with position, possession or achievements. She knows that possessions and status in society can be lost unexpectedly over night due to physical, social, political or economic changes which may occur at anytime, in spite of her personal effort and hard work. Therefore the secure woman in question is a woman who has found the secret to true security, which comes from that inner assurance and peace in knowing that God is for her and is in control. Her strongest weapon against uncertainty, anxiety and fear which are the number one enemies of security is found in Jer.29:11: "For I know the thoughts that I think towards you saith the Lord, they are thoughts of peace and not of evil, to give you an expected end."

She also knows from Prov.10:22; that "the blessing of the Lord maketh rich and He addeth no sorrow with it." **She trusts God.** In all her life experiences, she has this solid foundation that "All things work together for good to them that love God, and are called according to His divine purpose." The assurance that God is in control of her life brings such unspeakable peace, that in the face of any storm she boldly declares "The Lord is my light and my salvation whom shall I fear? The Lord is the strength of my life of whom shall I be afraid."

In no uncertain terms, the secure woman is a woman who takes God's word as it is and leaves no room for doubt or argument. She takes God at His Word for she is a woman whose strength is deeply rooted in God. For her, God's infallible and unchanging word is enough. Because of her deep faith in God, she is filled with such wisdom and knowledge about her personal worth that, she has a very balanced image of herself in the eyes of God and society.

She needs no extras in life to make her feel good about herself. I mean she doesn't depend on flatteries for impetus in life. She is a hardworking woman who has a very positive attitude towards life. Therefore, she sees the fruits of her labor and that gives her a personal sense of satisfaction. She is a good leader because she makes room for others to improve upon themselves without envy or strife. She challenges others to push forward in life without any feelings of threat to her position, ego or self-image. Truly, she lends a helping hand if one will only co-operate with her. She respects other people's decisions because she believes in others and appreciates their achievement without any feelings of jealously or regret of helping them. She is inspired unto greater heights by other people's good qualities and does not feel inferior or superior to any one. She believes in herself therefore, she can appreciate others and believe in them.

To the secure woman, her physical appearance is of great importance to her as well as her inner sense of peace and contentment. She has good sense and chooses colors and styles that present a very modest and descent appearance while affording her a great air of satisfaction, poise and grace. This is in sharp contrast to an insecure woman who tends to dress flambouyantly with excessive colors, and jewelry; whose dress code and appearance, is just to attract undue attention to herself.

The secure woman's normal posture while sitting, standing and walking speaks a lot about her inner quality and poise. She does not try to attract men's attention unnecessarily. She does not use too strong or offensive perfumes to attract people's attention unduly. She believes that although a man is responsible for his thought life, she will not allow herself to be the object of sinful thought by her lifestyle.

She gives wise counsel, for she is not given to prejudice. Oh what a wonderful character to be with! She is in great demand and very precious, for her price is far above rubies. She believes that "Favor is deceitful and beauty is vain, but a woman who fears the Lord, she shall be praised" Prov.31:30

In a nutshell, the secure woman's security has a lot to do with her spiritual position in God, which has invariably affected every facet of her life.

Her strongest anchor is found in Ps. 91: 1&2 "He that dwelleth in the secret place of the Most High shall abide under the shadow of the almighty. I will say of the Lord He is my refuge and my fortress, my God, in Him will I trust." In short, she knows God and is very content and understands divine insurance. That is, security in God for now and the future. She sees Psalm 91 as her divine Insurance Document. And she knows that as long as she remains under the canopy of God's Love and protection, walking daily in obedience to the inner promptings of the Holy Spirit, and heeding the voice of His Word, her life is forever "hid with Christ in God." Therefore whether she lives or dies, she lives and dies unto God. She is fearless, brave and strong. She is not threatened by challenges. By depending on God's strength, she intimidates her intimidators giving room for God's word to prevail in every circumstance of her life. She loves God and is very much assured of His Love for her. If you ever come across her, stick fast to her for her good qualities will surely rub off on you. Please look for her for it is possible that you could turn out to be the one we've been talking about. Lift faith up and declare, "I can do all things through Christ who strengthens me." And with a great deal of Faith, self-discipline and hard work your efforts will be rewarded.

CHAPTER TEN

THE INSECURE WOMAN

The Insecure Woman, who is she? The Insecure Woman is a woman whose foundation in life is unstable because it is not solidly built on the Rock, which is Jesus Christ the Word of God. She doesn't know how to walk with God. She is completely influenced by her five senses. Which means, what she sees, feels, smells, tastes' and hears' represents the fabric of her life. Her life seems to be tossed about on life's sea by waves from all sides. She doesn't seem to find any rest in her soul or heart.

It is very important to note that the insecure woman could be a Christian woman, even serving in the house of God, but she has not yet discovered the place of deep assurance of God's love and faithfulness. She is full of fear and uncertainty, which means she does not know how to walk in faith. Because of that, even though she is in service to God, her life does not please God because "without faith it is impossible to please God." (Heb 11:6)

The insecure woman does not know how to completely rely on the Word of God for protection and direction. Because of this, she is full of anxious thoughts and doubts about her future. She knows God is good and faithful to His child, at least that is what she has heard from the pulpit and read from the Bible, but she has not yet come to the place of complete trust. God's Word alone is not enough for her, she always seeks extra signs before feeling reassured to accept God's Word, which she usually does with the expectation of possible lose or failure. In short, the insecure woman is a faithless Christian. If she has any faith at all it is weak. The insecure woman is full of unnecessary regrets for her past, confused about her present and scared and uncertain about her tomorrow. She is so bound to her past experiences that she cannot look to the future with optimism.

Because of blunders done in the past, she does not even believe in herself anymore. She has lost her sense of self worth, and is therefore suspicious of people who try to get too close to her, for fear of being side stepped, overlooked or used. She easily gets hurt, wounded and dejected at the slightest show of resistance from anyone who seems to have a different opinion from hers. Her enemy is fault finding and she lacks appreciation of those that are better than her in any specific area, forgetting that she also has her God given and unique qualities that need to be explored and used. This same attitude creates in her, strife and envy, which drift people away from her. The insecure woman is therefore a lonely woman whose emotional imbalance reveals an individual who is ignorant of her self worth. The enemy uses ignorance to take advantage of her and make her exchange precious things in her life for the worthless because of her lack of appreciation for things that concerns her.

The insecure woman lacks the ability to take the initiative because of fear of failure. Her own dreams though many, lie dormant underneath the blanket of flimsy excuses and postponement while she looks on longingly at the fulfillment of other people's dreams. Her closest companion is procrastination. She believes that 'tomorrow' will always have a magic wand to wave over her dreams and aspirations, so that they will get fulfilled by themselves.

Sometimes due to her fear of rejection the insecure woman may go to extreme lengths to make undue sacrifices, without counting the cost, just to be accepted and feel loved by those she looks up to for recognition and appreciation, which leads to deep feelings of rejection and self pity when her expectations are not met.

The insecure woman may also try to cover up her weakness of inferiority complex with extremism in dress code just to attract people's attention and admiration. She is never satisfied with her God given beauty.

Oh what a pity! The strong desire to be loved and accepted has almost reduced this precious woman into a puppet, even though she may be very pretty and blessed with a lot of good qualities. One of these days she will wake up to the realization that God does not create nonentities or useless beings, and that her God has faith in her enough to entrust her with a few spiritual gifts and open opportunities for progress. Her day of increase and glory will come when she learns to appreciate what God has already given her and begins to explore her untapped potential by stepping out in faith, knowing that win or lose, God's Grace is that which enables her to accomplish her pursuits in life and therefore, giving the glory to Him, is the key to her freedom.

One major characteristics of the insecure woman is her self-centeredness. She has not learned Paul's secret "I can do all things through Christ who strengths me." Maybe her change will come when she begins to look into Gods word for the TRUTH about herself. When she discovers that, "If God be for us, who can be against us," her confidence will rise high. For her foundation to be firm and secure, she needs to know this; "Who shall separate us from the Love of Christ? Nothing, not tribulation or distress or persecution or famine or nakedness, or peril or sword, nay in all these things we are more than conquerors," the Bible says.

The insecure woman needs to remember that God's word is true and He never fails His children. "For God is not a man that he should lie, neither the son of man that he should repent, hath he said and shall he not do it, or hath he spoken and shall he not make it good?" Numbers: 23:19

The Bible says, "Heaven and earth shall pass away but God's word shall not pass away, it abides forever." Her breakthrough will come when she learns to believe in herself as an instrument in the hands of God. She must learn that she is precious and specially chosen by Him, for His Glory. An insecure wife will be a frustration for any man to live with because he will not receive the necessary help and encouragement needed to face the challenges of life for the fulfillment of his God given goals and visions. May the Lord open her eyes to behold wondrous things out of his law so that she can draw strength to hold her life together for the good of her family?

Many insecure women in the House of God will become a force for the enemy to reckon with if they can rediscover themselves in the light of God's Word and renew their personal sense of self worth. To be productive and full of substance, she will need the divine strength that comes from knowing her God in a more intimate way. This will result in her spirit being refreshed and filled with renewed assurance and faith to press on in life so that she can be a blessing to many.

The insecure woman does not have to be shut in under that label forever because she can make every effort to enter into that world of security and peaceful rest that only her personal faith in God and in what He has made her, can produce.

The Bible declares in Hebrews 4: 9-11, There remaineth therefore a rest to the people of God. For he that is entered into his rest, he also has ceased from his own works, as God did from his. Let us labour therefore to enter into that rest, lest any man fall after the same example of unbelief.

The above quote is an encouragement from God to the Insecure Woman to lean on Him, rest in His Love, and completely abandon her life to God in total surrender through her personal faith in the finished work of Jesus Christ, her Lord and master, who is King of all Kings and Lord of all Lords, for our God is the Father of all lights with whom is no variableness neither shadow of turning .She can totally depend on Him. He will never fail her! He is Jehovah Shalom! He is our Peace!

Precious Woman of God, Rest in the Lord!

CHAPTER ELEVEN

THE FRUITFUL WOMAN

The Fruitful Woman is the woman whose life giving source is Christ. She is full of life and vitality. Her heart condition is like the good soil in Jesus' parable of the sower. God's Word produces results in her life. She is a doer of the Word and not a hearer only. Because of this, her spiritual womb is always yielding abiding fruits to the Glory of God. It does not matter what 'weather conditions' her life circumstances may create for her. Be it in drought or rain, she has the ability to sustain the life giving seed established within her spirit through perseverance and faith. And to the Glory of God, she always emerges with rejoicing bringing in the sheaves, the fruits of her labor. The fruitful woman knows that toil and labor a part and parcel of sowing and investing in hard and difficult times. She knows the art of patient endurance during the waiting period of life, where faith and hope gives strength, until the time of joyful harvest!

She is a blessed woman because her labor and toil yields a harvest that brings nourishment and refreshing unto many famished and deprived souls. The fruitful woman is a woman of wisdom and foresight. She has a way of bringing life and light into any dead or dark situation. She is like a tree planted by the rivers of waters, which bears her fruit in season and out of season. She has thrown off all excuses that will make her fail in achieving her goals. She is a woman that is fully armed with new and applicable ideas for increased productivity. You can always count on her for a word or action that will meet you at the point of your need. The fruitful woman has her roots deeply rooted in Christ her life giving source.

The machinery upon which her life runs never seems to run out of fuel. She is fully equipped for life. "NO SHORTAGE" is the sign on her doorpost! She is a strong woman full of energy and power. Her reservoirs are filled with enough provision to meet the needs of weary pilgrims who pass through her home on life's journey. She is able to make do with that which God has provided, enough always to share.

The fruitful woman is a faithful servant and steward for God who has no reservations when entrusting his precious talent into her hands. He knows she will commit all her virtues into making His investment in her life a profit-yielding venture, with very high margins. She does not bury her talents in the sand, nor does she allow laziness and slothfulness to control her ways. She is a hardworking woman. She has no room for Idealness and she wastes no seeds, but invests them.

The fruitful woman is a productive woman who uses time wisely, always prepared for the rainy and stormy day. She is a woman of great achievement because she knows how to sow her seeds in good soil and wait patiently for the harvest, tending and caring for her plants. Let me share with you the spiritual background of the fruitful woman. In John, chapter Fifteen (15) verses 1 &2 we read, "I am the true vine, and my Father is the husbandman. Every branch in me that beareth NOT FRUIT He taketh away; and every branch that BEARETH FRUIT, He purgeth it, that it may bring forth MORE FRUIT." Now the fruitful woman being a woman of spiritual understanding knows from the passage above that in all her life experiences, the father has one purpose and that is to bring her to a prosperous state, a place of increase and productivity, a place where she can bear More Fruit to His glory.

She has discovered that there is a life that relates to the branch that beareth "NOT FRUIT", she completely avoids that and reaches out for the life that corresponds with the branch that BEARETH FRUIT, considering carefully that, this choice will attract the PRUNING KNIFE of the husbandman, with the divine purpose that she can graduate from BEARING FRUIT to BEARING MORE FRUIT!

Therefore after counting the cost, the Fruitful Woman comes to the place of total yieldedness unto God in complete trust, knowing that her difficult and challenging life experiences are not for her destruction but to bring her to a place of increased productivity where she can bear MORE FRUIT for the nourishment and blessing of God's children, and for the expansion of His Kingdom. Now you would think the fruitful woman will stop here with such great achievement but on the contrary, there is a greater and higher calling for which she desires above all else, and that is; BEARING MUCH FRUIT. In John 15:8 Jesus says: "I am the vine, ye are the branches. He that abideth in me, and I in him, the same bringeth forth MUCH FRUIT; for without me ye can do nothing. In this is my father glorified, that ye bear MUCH FRUIT; so shall ye be my disciples." Note that the emphasis here is ABIDING IN THE VINE, which is Christ, THE WORD OF GOD. For the Fruitful Woman therefore, an INTIMATE RELATIONSHIP' with Christ is the path way to that place of BEARING MUCH FRUIT. A place of increased production and overflowing abundance of life giving fruit to the glory of God.

In the human world, it takes the seed of a man in the womb of a woman to bring about productivity. Without the seed of the man in the woman, she cannot bear fruit. In much the same way, concerning Christ and His bride, she needs the seed of God's Word in her spiritual womb, that is her heart, where all life issues are born, (Pb: 4:23) so that through her continuous abiding in him for divine nourishment she can reach the point where her 'spirit man' will grow into full maturity, for divine increase and fruitfulness. In 1Peter2:2, the 'spirit man' in all of us is our human spirit and when it is recreated and born again, it requires the sincere milk of the Word of God as nourishment to grow. For Jesus said, "WITHOUT ME YE CAN DO NOTHING." (John15:5)

To the fruitful woman therefore her decision to abide in Christ is with the understanding that her entire life is completely entwined in the will of God. She is totally submissive to the Holy Spirit, who imparts the Spirit Life of God into her spirit through the rhema word. Her continuous fellowship with the Lord and her walk of obedience to His Word, through the strength of the Holy Spirit makes her bear fruits that ABIDE. When fruits are born in the flesh they cannot survive the spiritual challenges of life. "For that which is born of the flesh is flesh and that which is born of the spirit is spirit" and so they that are in the flesh cannot please God, for "The letter killeth but the spirit gives life." **And the Bible declares** "WALK IN THE SPIRIT and ye shall not fulfill the desires of the flesh." (Gal: 5:16) With this understanding, the fruitful woman knows her life is completely dependent on the nourishment she receives from a life of complete surrender to God's will.

The secret of her life and strength is an intimate walk with Christ. She leaves a positive and lasting impression on the lives of the people she affects. It is therefore not a wonder to notice that her life is filled with the reflection of Christ's beauty as she bears the fruit of the spirit, which is LOVE, JOY, PEACE, GENTLENESS, FAITH, HOPE, and KINDNESS AND SELF CONTROL. Note that these fruits can be imitated but never duplicated. These are spiritual fruits unique in quality and effect. By the spiritual fruits she bears, she has given birth to many souls for the increase of God's Kingdom. She knows how to die to self and live unto Christ, just for the purpose of bringing glory to the Father. The fruitful woman believes in investing her God given attributes into the lives of people who will also invest their lives into others for a continued Harvest.

At this point it is of great importance to understand that fruitfulness in this context is not referring to child bearing in the natural. For the fruitful woman may be a woman who has no biological children of her own due to certain natural reasons, yet her life is fully committed to taking care of God's children. She is a mother both to the young and old, and many lives have been positively affected through her hard work and selfless sacrifices.

She is a Social asset to her community because, many children have had their needs met and others have been blessed with good education, good food to eat, and clothes to cover their backs, for with her God given resources she affects her community positively, by helping to alleviate poverty and making life better for others. Through her hard work and positive attitude towards teamwork she is a great influence for good community development projects. She is indeed a blessing to Society.

The Fruitful woman is always looking for opportunities to give instead of taking or receiving. She experiences a special kind of joy and fulfillment when she can add something good to other people's lives, for her closeness and intimacy with Christ makes it easy to express the life of Christ to mankind through her love, care and devotion. She practices what she believes. She believes that faith without works is dead. James 2:14–17. Stay close to her for she has learned the secret to Devine Prosperity as revealed in Luke 6: 38; "Give, and it shall be given unto you; good measure, pressed down, and shaken together, and running over, shall men give into your bosom. For with the same measure that ye mete withal it shall be measured to you again."

Her store house never lacks provision for her source is God Himself .Isn't she a blessing to emulate? Her life is indeed a TRIBUTE to Christianity. Precious Ladies, this is the Portrait of a Fruitful Woman.

CHAPTER TWELVE

THE BARREN WOMAN

The Barren Woman is barren because of where she has spiritually positional herself. Jesus said, "Without me ye can do nothing." Her life is fruitless because she does not acknowledge God as her divine source. She is unfruitful in every aspect of life. She does nothing to bring increase or progress into her own life, nor that of her family or society. No one really benefits in anyway from her existence.

The barren woman is empty and dry. She does not have substance (unless she has acquired it through her 'natural resources'), because she is full of vanity. She can be easily detected in our social gatherings. She looks for opportunity to use her beauty or cunningness to turn, a man of substance and perhaps family, astray. A married man not fully centered in the Word of God is an easy target as he show's he is stable in most of His ways but is open to temptation from a beautiful glance and flattering words. She wants this man for her own personal gain. Such men end up used and reduced to paupers by the extravagant lifestyle of such a barren and fruitless woman, while their own wives and children languish in lack and want for the basic necessities of life, like a good home environment, well balanced and nutritious meals, good medical care, and payment of bills and school fees for a better future. All their resources will be drained into supporting the lifestyle of this barren woman. May the Lord deliver our young men, husbands and fathers from her lustful and destructive clutches!

She does not possess the seed of life, which is the ingredient needed for increase and productivity. She is like a cloud without rain. She forgets that the revealed and inspired Word of God in her heart, which is the seed of life, is that which will bring increase and fruitfulness into her life. She lacks wisdom and initiative and is a lover of material wealth, personal comfort, leisure and pleasure. She is lazy and full of excuses. It is not surprising that she does not miss an opportunity to receive or take from others while holding on tightly to her potential seeds of good will, which she could have sown or invested into other lives, for a good harvest in due season.

The barren woman is fruitless because she is self centered and greedy for material gain. She learned in school perhaps, that achievements are born out of perseverance, hard work, and great sacrifice. She however conveniently forgets that these principals apply to her as well. It is as if she believes she is owed a plush life itself and should not have to put anything in to it. She is cunning and foolish and enjoys the fruits of other people's labor holding tightly to her practiced excuses and reasons why she has no personal achievement. All of which I would like to add, is because she just so happens to place the blame for her lack of personal achievement, of course, on others. She accepts no responsibility for either her actions or the lack thereof.

She is also barren because of her fear to step out with faith and confidence in the stormy days of life. Therefore, all her good intensions are meaningless. Procrastination and a huge mountain of fear, has choked the opportunities for progress in her life. The barren woman is a coward at heart. She's timid and never ready for any eventualities in life. She has no sense of self-discipline and the results are continued confusion and defeat.

It is important to note that the barren woman may have biological children of her own but because of her deformed character may not be able to impart into them the good qualities that can prepare them adequately for life. She blesses no one, not even her own children, for they have no good example to emulate; and because they have no proper focus in life, they lack direction. These children inherit predation as a result of being influenced by her lifestyle of aimless, lazy, self-centeredness.

It is no wonder she cannot bear fruit because she has detached herself from the main stem of Gods Vine and therefore has become a withered and unfruitful branch. When tough times come her way, she quits, refusing to go the extra mile, thus yielding no fruitful results. This is because she lacks the inner quality of perseverance, which makes her give up under pressure even though she may be very close to her breakthrough.

Truly speaking, the closer to success she gets, the more willing she is to abandon the task and give it up. She wears her failures as badges of courage and they comfort her because they attract pity and some ones ear to listen. She would rather pacify herself by crying on others shoulders in the hope of someone else carrying her burden than put in the effort into accomplishing the task even in a minimal way.

Another major characteristic of the barren woman is waste. An example of her wasteful lifestyle is her use of Time. She places no value in time, even though it is a most precious ingredient in productivity when properly utilized. She is a daydreamer, with imaginations of beautiful things all locked up in a beautiful treasure chest in her beautiful mind, but to pay the costly price of hard work and toil to see her dreams fulfilled is a thing for the future. But for now, she waits patiently hoping and praying that her precious dreams will one day fall from the skies into her lazy lap for her easy consumption.

A married barren woman is a frustration to her husband. Especially if he is a good husband who knows how to sow good seed and gently tend and water it expecting, a bumper harvest. Yet with a little bit more love and firmness, he may be able with the help of God, to gently lift her off the plane of inactivity and fruitlessness to a place of activity and increased production. Whether married or single the Barren Woman needs to have an encounter with wise and purposeful women, so that she can glean a few essential lessons from them about life. She can be encouraged by the evidence of the fruits of their labor and she can submit herself to their wise and productive counsel which can propel and stir up her hidden potential that lies dormant under her lazy pile of excuses, or pushed under a heap of unfortunate life experiences.

It can be said that the world would be a better place with out the Barren Woman, looking at the devastating effect of her life style on the Society, and even though that is not God's purpose for her, if she does not change her life style, it might be so said of her. It is evident that the lack of accountability and responsibility in the barren woman has ended up causing the breakup of many marriages. This in turn has caused many poor children to find them selves living on the streets and at the risk of disease and death. They are often at the mercy of thieves, child abusers and pimps. This leads the children to perhaps the only method for their survival which is drug trafficking and addiction, prostitution and alcohol abuse. Above all, they become the jobless youth out there who have no profession or vocation in life. These situations can be turned around if this precious woman could add a little bit more sacrifice and hard work to her life instead of the laziness, ease and love of pleasure we see in her.

As previously pointed out, this woman would rather enjoy the fruits of other people's labor then expend the effort to have fruit of her own. She is filled with a lot of excuses like a broken marriage or wayward husband, lack of capital, or fear of failure if she steps out to make a difference on her own, and a huge pile of reason's why her life is not bearing fruit. Pushing the blame on others and on circumstances instead of accepting responsibility and making an effort to change her mentality and attitude is her stock in trade. She forgets that a thousand mile journey begins with a single step. She also forgets that to be able to reach out and see desires met, one has to pay the price of selflessness, persistence, hard work, with faith and hope even in the face of shame and failure. She needs to remember that,"she only has to succeed the very next time she tries to be a success. Don't try, and she guarantees failure." If she does not give up or give in under pressure she will eventually discover the way to success and fruitfulness.

To the barren woman I would say, do not accept the unfortunate position you are in now. Relocate yourself from defeat and fruitlessness by renewing your mind and your purpose in life. Acknowledge God as the giver of life and the source of all wisdom and strength, and add a good dose of hard work and determination to your faith. With perseverance and hope your faith will be rewarded and your life will experience change, increase and productivity. That is the road to fruitfulness and abundant blessings. May God help you and bless your good effort!

CHAPTER THIRTEEN

THE BEAUTIFUL WOMAN

The Beautiful Woman and the Wise Woman who we will discuss later are very similar in character because their foundation is built on the same thing: *"THE FEAR OF GOD"*

This woman's beauty does not have much to do with her physical features because she may or may not be physically attractive to look upon. There is an adage that says, "Beauty is in the eyes of the beholder." That may be true in one sense, but the kind of beauty we are about to discuss is one that is best described by Peter in 1Peter 3:3-4; it states, "whose adorning (beauty) let it not be that outward adorning (beauty) of plaiting or braiding of the hair, and of wearing of gold or of putting on of apparel (or fashionable clothing). But let it be the hidden man of the heart in that which is not corruptible (or subject to decay} even the ornament (beauty) of a meek and quiet spirit, which is in the sight of God of great price". This picture of a priceless gem in the sight of God is the foundation upon which the beautiful woman's life stands. Talking about mere physical beauty in a woman, the Bible declare in Prov. 31:30 that "Favor is deceitful and **beauty is vain**, but the woman that feareth the Lord she shall be praised."

A beautiful woman therefore is a woman whose life radiates the beauty of God's divine attributes. She's the embodiment of kindness, love, humility, and gentleness and a special sweetness and charm that can be best described as "captivating." She's full of wisdom and grace and the condition of being with her can best be described similarly to what David in Ps. 23, says: "He maketh me lie down in green pastures, He leadeth me beside **the still waters**, and He restoreth my soul." In other words, when you are with such a woman your life is **a continuous flow of peace, joy and tranquility**. She is God's gift to His creation, to make life on earth meaningful and fulfilling. She is the one Adam referred to as "Bone of my bone and flesh of my flesh." She is the fulfillment of every man's heart's desire. For she may be a wife a mother a sister a grandma, Aunt, Mother-in-law, friend, or maybe a boss lady or a brief acquaintance. But in all these instances, she has a way of touching your heart so deeply you find it difficult to take your mind off her.

She is as pure and refreshing as a cup of cold water on a hot and sunny day. She is full of humility and patience. She has a way of making you forget that life has a negative side to it. She is a woman whose heart condition is best revealed by the words of wisdom and kindness that flows freely from her lips. Let me take this opportunity to share with you some striking features of this beautiful creation of God. For she is the crowning joy of all God's creation, and brings satisfaction to His heart. God is proud of her and He respects her.

God's saving grace is beautifully set like a crown upon her queenly head and her hair is as smooth as silk. She is graceful. Her forehead unfretted by recrimination has a shinning glory that reveals the deep quality of loyalty, purpose and wisdom that the Holy Spirit alone gives.

Deep within her eyes reside pools of LOVE, PEACE, TRUST, PURITY, KINDNESS, AND UNDERSTANDING reflecting cool and refreshing acceptance and a willingness to be compassionate. Her ears are beautifully fashioned, eager to listen with patience and concern and they are ready for good counsel. Her nose is well patterned not to stick into others' affairs but positioned such that she can appreciate the sweetness of Gods world and breathe life into. These features reveal to you a life of obedience, good judgment and discernment.

Her lips are well shaped with the beauty of truth and the colors of life. Her mouth is full of laughter, songs of praise and encouraging words. It is likened to a beautiful rose, dripping with the sweetness of pure honey, which is wisdom and good counsel. Her arms are beautifully positioned by her side. They are never crossed in closed mindedness upon her bosom. In this fashion, she reveals their strength and readiness to labor and toil for the good of all mankind in selfless service. She reaches out her smooth and delicate hands to gently touch and apply the healing balm of God's care to the wounded and hurting without prejudice. She has enough room in her arms for all God's children. Her body has the posture of dignity and strength, which is a result of good nourishment from the milk and meat of the Word of God. Her heart vibrates with passion from a consistent life of prayer and sweet communion with her God. She truly loves and appreciates His Mercy. Her mind is peaceful and stable with no room for vain thoughts or evil imaginations. The deceiver hears His own voice echo back unaccepted for there is no place in her mind to receive His lies.

She has a clear conscience being assured of God's forgiveness and acceptance. This she reciprocates by an attitude of forgiveness and readiness to pardon her fellowman. Her graceful legs and feet are the very replica of a life of great balance and honesty, firmly established on truth, righteousness and integrity. Her feet never tread the path of falsehood and deception. She is pure and chaste. She loves sincerity; her heart is full of appreciation and joy for God's gift of life. The beautiful woman! Oh where will the world be without her, for she is a light to the world, and salt to the Earth? She makes the world a better place to live in. In times of fear and loneliness, her sweet voice of comfort flows like music into your ears bringing refreshing reassurance to your soul.

Her great sense of humor adds to her attraction. Her graceful looks and attractiveness are reflective of her God fearing attitude.

Her rare spiritual beauty is best revealed by her honest approach to life and her genuine and faithful spirit. She loves God and her expression of love to man are not just mere words. As a wife, she is the answer to every man's prayer and desire for "Who so findeth a wife findeth a good thing, (a beautiful woman) and obtains favor of the lord." She is the epitome of friendship in the marriage for she has all the qualities necessary for a true and deep relationship in marriage. She is as humble and peaceful as she is gentle and strong. She is a joy to live with. Nagging and complaining are not familiar with her; her words are full of faith and gratitude to God and to all her household. Peace is the best description of the atmosphere in her home and tranquility and rest is the bed her household sleeps on.

The food she sets on her table is called abundance and good health. It is set with grace and goodwill, as she never turns a stranger away. She shares all that God has given her. Her dessert is laughter and the fullness of life, which richly resides in her home.

She is a woman that is liberated from all emotional setbacks and her unique trait is that she is easy to be entreated. She is a lover of peace, which reflects her respectful and loving spirit. She is like the glue of God's creation, putting back together the broken pieces in man's life. To her husband, family or community, life cannot be the same without her. Her true beauty and inner quality shape her character and as a result, she has led many wayfaring men to the Shepherd of their souls, Jesus Christ, whose divine nature and life is clearly manifested in her. Her soul is beautiful it is mirrored by God's word in her mind, body, and spirit!

She is truly a beautiful human being and a credit to God's creation of the woman.

CHAPTER FOURTEEN

THE UGLY WOMAN

The ugly woman's physical features have little to do with our discussion because she may or may not be physically attractive but exhibit a very ugly and unrefined attitude. Her physical appearance means little to onlookers because of her repulsive character. Her heart is full of pride, contempt and resentment, which show in her mannerisms.

The ugly woman does not appreciate God's divine blessing of life and is never satisfied with what she has. Like the barren woman, she is greedy of gain and very covetous. She believes that every good and beautiful thing in life was meant for her. But because of her offensive attitude, goodness always passes her by leaving her wounded, and hurt. As a result she hates people with beautiful character traits, for their beauty seems to throw more light on her ugly character flaws and features.

The ugly woman is rude and quarrelsome. Her beauty is best described as "an ornament of gold in the snout of a pig." Her nagging voice is like "the dripping of water on a rainy day." With the little description we've had of the ugly woman, you would agree with me that she is not a pretty sight to behold. Neither is she a character one would love to be acquainted with in an intimate or lasting relationship. Married or unmarried, she is a pain to be with. You quickly look for a way of escape from her clutches.

She is loud and boastful, full of railing and cursing. She exaggerates to win arguments, or gain sympathy by pointing out how badly other people are treating her just to win acceptance. She has a manipulative character, scheming her way through life at the expense of other people's dignity, effort and labor. Yet she is quick to take the smallest of credit. She is deceptive and sly, cunning and crafty, and words, are her weapons. She is not courteous or kind in word, deed or expression unless it gains her something. As a married woman the ugly woman is a disgrace to her husband. She brings him no honor. Instead, she brings him humiliation with constant argument and disrespect sometimes publicly. Anger, frustration and rage are her closest companions. She is blunt and raw in her expressions, not considering the effect of her words and actions on people. She speaks her mind as if it is her right to do so even at the expense of others reputation and dignity. Therefore peace-loving people tend to avoid her company, for she is not really friendship material. She does not know how to keep secrets; she is a betrayer and can not be trusted. Yet the ugly woman could have been helped if she was humble and teachable but she hates reproof and correction. In her mind, she is never wrong. Her emotionally distorted life is her most identifiable trait for in her rage, she sometimes uses offensive language to berate the object or person of her rage. When she disciplines a child, she tends to be overly abusive as her rage takes over and her common sense leaves her.

She has the unfortunate habit of prolonging trivial matters, turning and twisting them into major issues, which makes her physical facial features (even if beautiful) expressive of her mind set and very, very detestable.

The ugly woman has no sense of humor because she is so insecure and full of explosive tantrums. She is like a spoiled child living in an adult's body. Even though she is quick in making friends through her forwardness, she quickly loses them because of the startling discoveries they make about her ugly character.

Understanding and peace making are alien to her because she sees them as a sign of weakness, and very humiliating to her ego.

The ugly woman does not want to come to terms with her true image because it embarrasses and intimidates her. It is difficult for her to admit her faults, and never takes responsibility for her mistakes and errors.

She causes a lot of heartbreak and pain to the people who love her, making life with her a very big challenge to them. She has lost many great opportunities in career advancement and many good friends because she lacks the social graces of humility and the good qualities of forgiveness and peace. She sacrifices her life at the expense of her opinions, even if they are totally wrong. She has forgotten the best adage of all: "If you cannot say something nice (and uplifting) it is better to say nothing at all."

Her attitude makes life with her a very boring exercise, as it is usually one argument after another. She does not know how to sacrifice or over look her personal interests of always being right; even at the expense of a good and lasting relationship. When she gets into her outrageous moods she lashes out bitterly with sharp words, creating deep wounds in the hearts of people whom she believes have offended her, even though she knows they love her. Her lack of sympathy and understanding makes her look even uglier for having her own way and avenging herself on her enemies, gives her great joy and deep satisfaction. She is very argumentative and would rather defend herself when she makes a mistake than accept it and receive correction, or learn from the experience.

Wise counsel and rebuke is only accepted if it gains her favor and acceptance. It doesn't mean she will act favorable upon it, only listen to it. Even so, she will attempt to justify her position through placing the blame on circumstance or someone else. She is always ready to add innuendo and supposition in vague reverences like "they said or everyone tells me the same thing, or nobody likes me, or if you only knew how everybody thinks" to add weight to her argument and slander.

She is insecure, a coward at heart and greedy of dishonest gain. Her lack of truth and decency makes women with beautiful character her enemies, whom she sees as a threat to her own identity. She hates competitive situations because the deformity in her character makes her feel very insecure with people who practice good conduct. She sees people with beautiful and attractive characters as opponents who must be put in their place, always below her self.

She is an unhappy woman full of ugly and evil thoughts and imaginations. She looks for any reason to twist a situation into an accusation, especially if she thinks the other person is trying to acquire help from her, which she is not ready to give. She always looks for the negative side of every situation. The ugly woman is a lonely woman. She is a pity to behold for her home is a place of chaos, confusion and warring words. Peace has no place to settle in her home. Many potentially good husbands have had their wonderful characters deformed by her constant arguing, nagging, complaining and dishonoring. She is so ungrateful and so full of venom that her life is a liability to the Kingdom of God.

She does not have the patience, humility and care necessary to gently guide the wayward in. Instead her attitude drives a person in the opposite direction. She has put many people off and pushed them away from the door of salvation due to her resentful attitude and negative presentation of Christianity by her life style. She has become a stumbling block to many wandering souls who should have found their way to eternal life if only she had been a little cooperative and considerate of them. This has made her Christian testimony a disgrace to Christianity and a discouragement to others, making no contribution to the Kingdom of God. She has become a source of grief to the HOLY SPIRIT, for he has NO ACCESS through her life to reflect the Beauty of God's love to a lost and dying world.

She has taken the false attitude that she hears the Holy Spirit and is in constant communion with God. But, the Bible teaches us, to "know them by their fruits," and anyone can judge for themselves how far away she is from God's Heart.

The ugly woman is an unfortunate example of womanhood, but her life can experience a transformation through the gentle and tender loving care of the beautiful woman if she opens up her heart ready for good counsel in complete humility for positive change. All she needs to do is accept her faults, failures and the fruit of her mistakes, and form good habits consistent with the Word of God. For good works always follows true repentance. And that is what she needs; Repentance, Reformation and Restoration from the Presence of God.

Her lonely and troubled life will then experience the Transformation needed to bring Peace and Tranquility into her life, and make her a blessing to all her loved ones and acquaintances, so that she can experience a happy and fulfilled life to the Glory of God. May the Lord help her! Amen.

CHAPTER FIFTEEN

THE WISE WOMAN

The Wise Woman is a blessing to the kingdom of God, and a good example to womanhood. Her wisdom in this respect does not refer to human ideologies or methods. For the Woman we are about to meet is one who is filled with divine insight and understanding into God's dealings with man and His expectations and plans concerning His children including herself.

The Wise Woman is the woman who acknowledges the Sovereignty of God, and her need for His wisdom and counsel to guide her life onto the paths of success and blessing. She is a woman who is very conscious of her worth to God, in spite of her failures and mistakes.

"The fear of the Lord is the beginning of Wisdom" therefore the wise woman is one whose foundation is firmly established on the fear and reverence for God and His Word. She cares to know God's opinion concerning her every life situation. She respects and honors God in every aspect of life. She carries with her the good qualities of gratitude and thankfulness for God's many blessings, which she experiences daily in her life. She is a woman who cares to know her spiritual state in the eyes of God. Fearing God for the wise woman does not mean running away from Him in terror, but walking daily in His presence with deep devotion and reverential fear considering His awesome Power, Majesty and Holiness.

She is a woman of immense understanding into spiritual things and of deep insight and revelation knowledge. For this reason, before she opens her mouth, in wisdom she considers the effect of her words on her hearers. She is very considerate and kind, with a word in season for every occasion or situation. Her words are like apples of gold on platters of silver. Her words are savory, seasoned with salt. Her words bring light to the shadows of fear, rejection, and disappointment.

She is wise because she sees God as her source of strength and blessing. She does not depend on her own understanding neither does she use her beauty or position to manipulate or control people. She is a good investor in time using it wisely to bring increase and enrichment into her life and all those she affects.

Depending on the counsel and direction of God, she orders her life in the paths of blessing and peace. Her wisdom is not of this world, filled with schemes and trickery, but deriving strength from her knowledge of God's will, she pursues His Will to the fullest. The wise woman's home is not controlled by her emotional instabilities creating confusion and frustrations for her household, but through her dependence and reliance on God's divine strength, she has learned how to submit her emotional life to the Holy Spirit, with patience receiving His transforming power through the Word of God.

The wise woman really builds her house on the Rock. She is smart and fully equipped for the wiles and strategies that the enemy tries to manifest through her human nature. She is sober, alert and steadfast in faith. She takes God at His word, leaving no room for doubts, fear or uncertainties. When her canal nature comes in conflict with the Word of God, she knows how to allow God's Word to take its rightful place in her life for a deep work of transformation, bringing glory to God and defeating the purposes of the enemy. Oh what manifestation of wisdom and prudence, for the wise woman's wisdom delivers her from the traps and temptations of the enemy, she places priority on spiritual and eternal things knowing that physical and materials things are temporary.

The wise woman understands purpose and destiny. Walking with God according to divine understanding is her delight. Because she believes that God is her defense, she never takes matters into her own hands by using her own defensive strategies to prove her case in any conflict situation. She rather waits on the Wisdom and Divine Judgment of God which always turns out better than her own human efforts, which for others not as wise, normally ends in defeat and shame. She trusts in the faithfulness of God.

In all things, she does not allow her emotions to stand in the way of the Holy Spirit. She believes that "Wisdom is better then weapons of war." That is why her marriage is a testimony, a delightful experience and adventure to her husband and a blessing to her children. Oh wisdom is indeed a divine legacy for prosperity. What fulfillment and joy she brings to those who find her and live by her. For her price is far above rubies and her merchandise than fine gold, she is so precious nothing can be compared unto her.

The wise woman has enough faith and virtue to withstand every life situation that rises to oppose the word of God in her life. And believe me, she always emerges victorious. The wise woman is abreast with the information of God's dealings in her life; therefore she is never overtaken by sudden events. Her life is a constant flow of God's Life Giving Grace and Wisdom that strengthens the life span of her relationships making her a delight to be with. She believes that by dying to self, she can reach out for more of God, which is the key to her victory over the enemy in all negative circumstances. The wise woman is a woman of foresight and vision for She knows what she wants and goes for it in spite of the obstacles, provided it is in line with God's purpose and plan for her life. She has a standard set for life, with principles that she will never compromise for anything less. She knows how to depend on God to turn hopeless situations around into positive and successful opportunities. The Wisdom of God produces creativity in her heart, enabling her to make the right and fruitful decisions that always results in blessings upon her and her loved ones.

The Wise Woman is a woman whose foundation is built upon her obedience to the Word of God and her relationship with Jesus Christ, the Rock of her Salvation.

Proverbs 14:1 states, *"Every Wise Woman buildeth her House, but the foolish plucketh it down with her hands"* This verse is the secret to the Wise Woman's fear and reverence for God which describes her as Wise in her role as wife and mother for the strength and support of her Household.

In Psalm127:1a, the Bible declares *"Except the Lord Build the House, they labor in vain that build it ..."* And in Jesus parable of the two builders ,a vivid description is given of the method they used in laying the foundations for the house they built and the results that emerged after the Testing period of Trial.

From the above verses we learn the main secret of the Wise Woman's Success in life is total dependence on God as the Wise Master Builder of her Life .She does not depend on the promises of man. No wonder her life is such a blessed Testimony to the Glory of God. The evidence of her wisdom is revealed in the manner in which she conducts her life.

In marital problem situations, the Wise Woman does not open up her private life to people who may pose as friends because she wants to win their sympathy or support. She considers carefully the fact that, to set her husband up for ridicule or shame is to destroy the Spiritual covering of her Family, which can affect her household negatively.

Despite the fact that she may have been wronged and therefore feel justified in sharing her problems with friends, the Wise Woman determines to walk by the principles of God's Word concerning her marriage, even though it may cost her, her Pride as a woman or her rights as a human being.

When her ability to handle her marital problems gets out of hand, she takes to the instruction of Mathew18:15-17, where she is instructed to seek godly counsel from the Spiritual Leaders God has set over her in the Church, or from qualified and reputable Christian Marriage Counselors.

She believes that God is concerned and involved in every detail of her domestic and private life and has the ability to take care of every situation she presents to Him in humble trust. With this attitude of faith and submission to God, she never loses a battle but always emerges victorious because her God fights her battles for her.

As stated in Jeremiah 17:5a, the Wise Woman has learned that "Cursed is every man who puts his trust in man" and from John 2:24-25 'Jesus Christ did not commit Himself to any man for He knew what was in man." With this knowledge she understands that to put her trust in man or depend on the judgment of man is to walk in deception and failure.

The Wise Woman's Life Foundation is built on these virtues; Patience, Tolerance, Long suffering, Compassion, Understanding, Endurance and Foresight, the summation of which is called ...Wisdom!

Her closest companions are Love and Peace, and with these virtues she conducts her life in a very peaceful and confident manner that makes people wonder if she ever faces challenges in life!

Indeed the Fear of The Lord is His Treasure; and where these Treasures are concerned, her heart is full of them!

CHAPTER SIXTEEN

THE FOOLISH WOMAN

"The fool hath said in His heart, there is no God." Ps. 53:1. The foolish woman's image is the direct interpretation to the verse above. One could wish that this type of woman had no living example on earth. But unfortunately, it is very sad to say that she does. The absence of woman from God's initial act of creation made him declare His work as incomplete, for God said; "IT IS NOT GOOD that the man should be alone, I will make him a helper suitable for him." This meant that the creation of the woman was the crowning event to God's process of creation. Therefore the fact that there is a woman today who refuses to acknowledge the existence and Sovereignty of God, by her life style speaks volumes to how really foolish she is which brings great sadness to the loving heart of God because His good plans for her life cannot be realized if she continues in this trend.

Like Eve of old, she has decided to depend on her own wisdom and judgment concerning the details of her life, by giving heed to the deceiver and enemy of her soul. To her, depending on God's counsel and plan for her life is a waste of her time. In her opinion, it is a thing meant for ignorant women who do not know what to do with their lives. Oh what a pity, for she is ignorant of the fact that without God's divine love and foresight, which caused Him to declare woman victorious over Satan in the garden of Eden even after the disobedience of Eve, women would have been held in bondage and subjection to the curse of sin, for the rest of their existence on earth.

But thanks be to God who in His divine Wisdom and predetermined counsel provided a way of escape for the woman and her descendants through the incarnation, crucifixion and resurrection of Christ, sealing mankind's eternal Destiny by His intercessory ministry in heaven seated at the right hand of the Father, and executing His counsel in our lives through the Power and presence of His Holy Spirit. The Foolish Woman is completely ignorant of these amazing truths, or otherwise, has no desire to walk in them, being deceived.

Yes, through Christ who is "The seed of the woman" in accordance with God's original promise" The seed of the woman shall bruise your head and you shall bruise His heel." Every woman needs to come to the beautiful and wonderful realization that God's desire and plan is for her well being, which requires a level of gratitude and appreciation that should make her bow in reverent worship and acknowledgement of His existence and sovereign power, so He can execute His Purposes and plans in and through her submissive life.

Unfortunately this precious woman has fallen back into Satan's original trap of suspecting God's faithfulness and ability to help her deal with her challenges in life, thus ignoring God and following her own pattern for life. This attitude has led this potentially prosperous and victories woman into a state of defeat, lack and shame. To go on in life ignoring God, His will and pattern for one's life, is like purchasing an electronic equipment from a manufacturer and refusing to accept the manual for its properly prescribed operation. You will surely end up with a completely, malfunctioning and broken down piece of equipment. Surely this attitude is that which makes this woman foolish because she has ignored the One who has the blue print for her life. No wonder her life condition of disgrace, confusion and despair is a clear evidence of reliance on the decisions of her own heart, which the bible describes as "deceitful above all things and desperately wicked.' Therefore, to depend on one's own heart is a sure way to fall into the trap of a deceived and confused life.

The Foolish Woman is an ignorant woman who does not treasure the counsel and wisdom of God that can make her wise for a fruitful and meaningful life. She is presumptuous, self-centered and demanding. Being completely deceived and trapped into believing that to enjoy life to the fullest, is to gratify every sensual and canal desire within her, leaves her spiritually bankrupt of every blessed virtue and glory that God had intended for her life. Through her ignorance and rebellion she places no value on Eternal issues. To enrich her life by any godly means, using such concepts as goodness or kindness is ok as long as it will give her gain and require no cost or commitment on her part whatsoever. To her, happiness and joy is derived from the favorable conditions she can create around herself even if she steps on many toes or push others down in the process. She is arrogant, proud and boastful attributing her successes in life to her own dubious efforts and schemes.

The Foolish Woman is misinformed about life, being ignorant of the fact that life has meaning and purpose only when it is a blessing to others who need her help. Like Esau, she is very short sighted and limited in spiritual understanding ready to exchange her "birthright for a morsel of bread," if only it will bring her immediate pleasure and satisfaction.

The Foolish Woman's greatest weakness is that she is too emotional and full of suspicion. Instead of focusing on how to change her negative attitudes during marital conflicts, she resorts to spiritualizing the situation and pushing the blame on demonic activity instead of submitting herself to God's word and good Christian counsel, for positive and constructive change in her character and attitude.

This attitude puts a great strain on her relationship with her husband and household. For this woman, wisdom waits patiently until the day she wakes up to face the reality of her unfortunate situation. Yes, the day, she will run after reproof and correction with a good degree of open mindedness. This will mark the beginning of healing in her life and relationships, which will in time manifest in a restored life of Joy and Peace.

The Foolish Woman's use of time, and resources has made her loose many great and rewarding opportunities but she will recover her wasted years when she begins to acknowledge God and depend on His divine counsel and plan for her life, marking the beginning of a wonderful journey where abundant life, peace, joy and blessings abound.!

If you acknowledge that the mirror of God's word in your heart reflects all that you have seen in these pages, then to break the bondage of Satan on your soul and life requires that you humble yourself to God and ask for His forgiveness, pray the sinner's prayer. Confessing your sins and repenting of them, you must believe that you are now forgiven and receive Jesus into your heart as your Lord and Savior. As you begin this wonderful journey and process of knowing Him and His purpose for your life, you will receive His wisdom and strength through the revelation of His Word which will change your life positively. And, your life will be enriched, by the people God places in your way as you also become a blessing to others through your new relationship and position in Christ.

Welcome into the Family of God. A new life of Peace, Excitement and Victory awaits you! Stay, in His Love.

CHAPTER SEVENTEEN

THE BLESSED WOMAN

This Precious Woman is blessed because she knows God. She is a woman that is hungry for God and is therefore filled with the fullness of His blessings.

She is like a life giving vessel in His hand, through which he expresses His beauty and love to His creation. The blessed woman is one who knows she is blessed and does not hold back any opportunity to be a blessing. She is pure in heart, peace loving, and without anxiety, for she is one who has learned the secret of casting her cares upon the Lord. The Blessed Woman is so humble and loving that she leaves no room for strife or confusion in her relationships, because she is very respectful and courteous. She is a lady. Her inner beauty expressed through her gentleness, sincerity and kindness makes her a very unique individual. No matter how discouraged you may be in life, this precious lady has the gift of restoring your self-confidence and faith to the point where your strength is renewed to go on in life with a more positive attitude.

Her presence in any family or society makes it stands out as an exception very much affected by her positive influence. The blessed woman possesses all the good qualities that every man would desire to have in a wife, she is really beautiful inwardly, full of the rich ingredients of forgiveness, understanding and a good sense of humor. The blessed woman is a God fearing woman whose Christianity needs no questioning, because her rich spiritual walk with God is clearly evident by the good fruits she bears in character.

She is neat and descent in appearance, very modest and not given to extravagance. She doesn't believe that poverty is piety, but rather, she works with her hands to assist her family in meeting their daily needs. She is not sluggish or lazy, but believes that her gifts and natural abilities have been given her by God to invest or utilize for the service of mankind.

She is disciplined and principled, a woman of good morals, not lustful or seductive. She believes that her physical beauty has been given her by God to bring glory to His name; therefore her life goal is to draw all men unto God through her inner beauty which reflects the nature and character of Christ.

She is very careful and uses a lot of discretion in her choice of friends, because she knows that friends have a way of influencing one's conduct in life. I'll-mannered people are often challenged to reconsider their life styles as they notice the good qualities she portrays. She has a way of seeing good in a bad situation, because her presence in the life of a sad or unhappy person brings immediate transformations of joy and assurance of God's Love thus producing Peace, because of the beautiful charm, kindness and gentleness, with which she communicates God's Loving Grace.

She is blessed because her feet does not lead her into trouble, but rather her love for peace and goodness makes her very courteous and respectful. She is not greedy or covetous but very satisfied with her God given resources and blessings, believing that Godliness with contentment is great gain. 1Tim. 6:6. She does not easily follow the crowd if she is not sure of the source or outcome of a thing, no matter how good it seems. She believes in laboring with her own hands, so that she can become a source of blessing to those in need.

She is pure and gentle in character, for bitterness and hatred have no room in her heart. Her life is the kind that brings joy to the heart of God and man. The blessed woman does not use her physical beauty to entice men, but lives a very descent and modest life. She goes out of her way to assist and support the wounded and hurting, gently guiding them through the good counsel of God's word. She is indeed a true example of God's desire and purpose for creating woman, for she is God's prepared vessel through whom He reveals His love and beauty to mankind.

God is truly proud of her, knowing that she will always bring him glory. She avoids situations or life styles that bring shame to God, for she has covenanted with Him to live her life on earth to glorify His name. No wonder, she is the source of Joy and Salvation unto many. Her local church or assembly is filled with zealous people full of good deeds, because of her exemplary life of giving and dedication. She loves the Lord and spends more time meditating in His word than on vain and shameful imaginations. The blessed woman is a woman who may not have had a very pleasant past, but like the apostle Paul; she has learned the secret of forgetting her past and pressing on towards the mark of the high calling of God in Christ Jesus.

She has a sweet and loving spirit that is ever ready to forgive and restore a broken relationship, even if she is the one that has been wronged. Because she appreciates God's forgiveness of her sins, she bears no man any grudge. She has a way of influencing you to do the right things and make the right decisions in life. She is a blessing to Christianity and a crowning joy to God's work of Salvation.

The blessed woman is a wonder unto many who marvel at what the source of her strength and beautiful qualities could be, she directs them to her secret place, under the shadow of His love. The place where he has prepared His vessels through out the generations of men, using them as carving tools in His hands to mould and shape the destinies of people and nations. To the blessed woman, life would have been meaningless if she had not been an available and prepared vessel to be used in the service of mankind. Her most blessed quality is her readiness to go the extra mile, just to bring glory to God. Her zeal for God is equivalent to the five wise virgins who took their burning lamps and an extra jar of oil, to handle any delays or eventualities. Her attitude of unreserved service and devotion to God and to men, has won for her this statement of praise; "Many daughters have done virtuously but thou excellest them all; give her of the fruit of her hands, and let her own works praise her in the gates. Proverbs 31:29-31. She is blessed and beautiful; she is indeed a virtuous woman, filled with the fullness of God and the abundance of His Blessing.

CHAPTER EIGTHEEN

THE CURSED WOMAN

It is of great importance for us to understand, before we proceed in our discussion of this character, that the Word 'Cursed' here, does not refer to a curse that has been placed on some one's life by merit, either through one's own mistakes or that of forefathers in their time of ignorance. For the bible says that "if any man be in Christ, he is a new creature" 2Cor. 5:17 and Christ has redeemed us from the curse of the law being made a curse for us". Therefore, all those who are of faith have been blessed with faithful Abraham.

Considering God's act of mercy through the work of Salvation, and in reference to the Bible verses above, we can conclude that God has made provision for man's salvation and deliverance from any known curse through the blood of Jesus Christ, and His finished work on the cross. By His resurrection those who believe are exalted to a position of authority and blessing. Therefore through the knowledge of God, and by the proper application of His word, the Prayer of faith can reverse every known curse, for "ye shall know the truth and the truth shall set you free" and He whom the son (Jesus; the truth) sets free, is free indeed. There is therefore no legal spiritual reason for us to live under a curse after Salvation, if we are living and walking daily in obedience to God's word. Who then is the Cursed Woman in our discussion?

The Cursed Woman we are referring to is one who has encountered the love and mercies of God, but has refused to acknowledge, God's divine work of grace and decided to continue living her life without God. To such a woman the blood of Jesus and His sacrificial death on the cross for her sins does not mean a thing. She only looks for an easy way of escape out of the challenges of life, even if it means resorting to idols or lesser gods, which are an abomination unto God, her creator.

She is a woman who through greed and covetousness has given herself wholly to the world, falling into the snare and trap of the devil, the enemy of her soul. The cursed woman is a strange woman; she is one who dabbles in the evil practices of occultism and witchcraft, for she eats the bread of wickedness and drinks the wine of violence. Her paths do not lead to life or peace, but to pain and death. When she goes to Church, it is only to cause mischief, for she is a slanderer and a gossiper, who brings confusion and factions into God's household. Tale bearing and lying are some of her most effective weapons of bringing defeat to the people of God. She is a breeder of contention among close friends, causing bitterness in their hearts thus defiling the people of God, and reducing their effectiveness and power, so that she can create a more conducive atmosphere of strife for her demonic operations. Watch out for her, people of God, for she may be close by. Please, live right, rebuke and expose her and if possible deliver her.

Perverseness is her closest companion deceiving and being deceived her end is always regret and emptiness, marked with the consequences of her rebellious life style, which are reproach, shame, poverty and spiritual death. .She lives her life for the satisfaction of sensual pleasures, and does not care what effects her desire for pleasure may have on other people's lives, and so many people have become victims of her careless lifestyle. An example is her enticement of married men, who end up ignoring their own wives and neglecting their parental responsibilities to their own children. Thus creating unfortunate situations like divorce, school dropouts and financial strains on family budgets, due to her extravagance and outrageous demands. She has no sense of shame when it comes to debasing her self for canal gains. Indeed, she is a shame to womanhood. Her closest companions are lewdness, pretence and wickedness. She is cunning and crafty believing in the deception of her foolish heart. She scoffs and makes mockery of things pertaining to God. She has no fear or reverence for God Almighty.

She is a strange woman indeed. The Cursed Woman through her deceptions winks her eyes and shuffles her feet and wriggling her body through the streets, turns away simple men who lack understanding and hates instruction, leading them into calamity, poverty, pestilence and untimely death. Her enticing package is full of dangers like AIDS, STD strange deceases and early loss of man hood. Do not yoke with her, for she is treacherous, and her house leads straight into hell. May our young men escape her traps and tentacles of false charm and deception, and our young ladies escape her enticement to follow in her footsteps.

To the cursed woman anyone can be an easy prey if only she is given the needed attention, she has no respect for dignity neither does she acknowledge natural relationships she is completely sold out to the devil increasing the population of hell through her lewd ness.

Let's see how the bible describes her in proverbs 5:3-6 and 8-14. "For the lips of a strange woman drop as an honey comb, and her mouth is smoother then oil, but her end is bitter as worm wood, sharp as a two edged sword. Her feet go down to death; her steps take hold on shoel"—- lest thou shouldest ponder the path of life, her ways are unstable that thou can't not know them. Remove thy way far from her house, lest thou give thine honour unto others and thy years unto the cruel, lest strangers be filled with they wealth and thy labours be in the house of an alien, and thou mourn at the last when thy flesh and thy body are consumed {Through what? AIDS?}, and say how have I hated instruction, and my heart despised reproof; and have not inclined mine ear to them that instructed me! I was almost in all evil in the midst of the congregation and assembly.

With reference to the last verse, we can notice that the strange woman can sometimes worm her way into a Church congregation or Christian assembly and try her deceptive and enchanting ways on the servants of God. Watch out Christian young men, and be sober Christian young ladies, for her demonic presence can manipulate and influence you into error, lest you become puppets and tools for her to use against the cause of your God. Watch what you see, and hear in Church and don't imitate blindly.

As Christian men and women if she gets you entrapped the bible has this to say; "Deliver thyself like a roe, from the hand of the hunter, and like a bird from the hand of the fowler. Proverbs 6:5. The Bible in no uncertain terms warns us to flee from her lustful and enchanting eyes. But even for the strange and cursed woman God has made a way for her escape from Satan's tentacles and control. And that is to acknowledge her sinful and wicked ways, turn around in true repentance, accept the forgiveness of God and make Jesus Christ the Lord of her life turning her back completely to her evil life style. Otherwise, like her Bible counterpart Jezebel, God has this warning in Rev. 2:20-23. **PARAPHRASE** *"Forbidding her from teaching and seducing His servants to commit fornication and to eat things sacrificed to idols, God gives her space to repent or else He will cast her into a bed of affliction, into great tribulation and will kill her children with death. So that the churches will know that it is He who searches the minds and hearts and will give unto every one according to their works."*

Isn't she dangerous, and isn't she a problem to the cause of God? But even to this cursed woman, God gives space to repent. Oh the love and mercies of God and the riches of His grace, they are unsearchable!

I pray that any woman caught in this wicked web of the devil will take God's counsel, and run to him for help, so that she can be spared the judgment determined. It is important to note that this character has affected the work of God down through the ages. Some servants of God escaped her craftiness whilst others fell victim to her cunningness. Let's name them. Delilah and Samson. Potiphar's wife and Joseph, Jezebel and Jehu. Herodias the wife of Philip, Herod's Brother, who asked for the head of John the Baptist on a Silver platter. Athaliah, the daughter of Ahab and Jezebel, who destroyed the seed royal of Judah in the days of King Joash, and Job's wife.

These strange women allowed Satan to use them to oppose the work of God, but none of them escaped judgment. Nevertheless, it is beautiful to note that there are examples of strange women in the bible who repented gave their will and lives to God for His divine transforming love and power to turn them from their rebellious state into a life filled with God's Glory and based on covenant relationship. Examples are: "Rahab the harlot, Ruth the Moabite, The woman caught in the act of adultery, Mary Magdalene and the woman at Jacob's well near Samaria.

In our modern day and time many such women, have risen from a past life of shame and defeat, rebellion and disobedience, into a place of sweet submission to God and His purpose for their lives. It is the heart cry of God, that none should perish, but that all such women will understand His love and reach out to him for mercy forgiveness and Restoration.

Well, ladies this calls for fervent prayer, doesn't it? So help us God! Amen.

CHAPTER NINETEEN

THE HUMBLE WOMAN

To open this chapter, we would like to look at some very important bible verses that best introduces this blessed woman. In Isaiah 66: 1a & 2b, the bible declares "Thus saith the Lord; the heaven is my throne, and the earth is my footstool... but to this man will I look even to him that is poor and of a contrite spirit and tembleth at my word". From this declaration of God, we can safely conclude that we are about to discuss and share about a woman whose commendation from God places her in a very enviable position. She is one to whom God, the almighty looks, His eyes run to and fro through out the whole earth to show himself strong on her behalf.

She is a woman who compels even God to stoop down to acknowledge her, not considering His dignity and Majesty. He says to this woman will I pay attention and consider. Therefore the big question is, the humble woman who is she? And what is the thing that makes her so unique and special.

The bible says three specific things about her in the above verses, which we would like to consider; first of all, the bible describes her as 'poor' of a contrite spirit and one who "trembleth at my word."

Now, you would agree with me that the word 'poor' in this verse does not refer to poverty in the sense of wealth or lack of material possession but like Jesus said, Blessed are the poor in spirit for theirs is the kingdom of Heaven.

This powerful statement means that this woman has authority before the throne of God, because she acknowledges her need for God and longs for more of him. I believe her greatest bible verse is Ps. 42: 1&2 *"As the hart panteth after the water brooks, so panteth my soul after thee Oh God, My soul thirsteth for God, for the living God; when shall I come and appear before God."* The last expression of the humble woman in the above verse is one of a longing and desire for God that best suits the condition of her heart. The question "When shall I' reveals her very desperate need for God, with a consuming passion that relates well with Jesus' statement. "Blessed are they who hunger and thirst after righteousness, for they shall be filled." From this verse we can deduce that the humble woman is a candidate for a life filled with the fullness of the Holy Spirit. Now our next point of reference is God's expression and of a contrite spirit contriteness in this context refers to an attitude of humble acceptance of her spiritual unworthiness before God. The humble woman knows that she does not deserve the mercies of God bestowed upon her, therefore she approaches the throne with awe and with reverence. Her inner qualities though many are not enough to make her feel that she deserves God's blessing and goodness. She rather looks for better ways to enhance her relationship with him.

Where as the proud woman makes a list of excuses and reasons why she makes mistakes or fall into mischief, pushing the blame on others, the humble woman on the other hand quickly accepts her faults and taking responsibility for her mistakes, repents and makes the necessary corrections removing all hindrances between her and God, so that she can have a clear conscience in serving Him. In Heb. 10:21-22 the bible says: - And having an high priest over the house of God, let us draw near with a true heart in full assurance of faith, having our hearts sprinkles from an evil conscience, and our bodies washed with pure water let us hold fast to our faith without wavering'.

From what we've studied so far the humble woman knows that her relationship with God is based on the attitude of her heart, and her faith in His word. She remembers that God is spirit and so to worship him in spirit and in truth is acceptable to Him. She also knows that God looks on the heart and so He knows a heart that is contrite and repentant she therefore leaves no room for compromise in her relationship with God. Her closest companions are gratitude, sincerity, loyalty and faithfulness. She is completely sold out to God.

In appreciation for the love and favor bestowed on her by God She declares with the Psalmist; in Ps. 8:3 & 4." When I consider they heavens, the works of thy fingers, the moon and the stars, which thou hast ordained, what is man that thou art mindful of him and the son of man that thou visitest him" she really appreciates God's love.

Now let us consider some of her qualities. The humble woman is sober and gentle. Her exceptional conduct and sincere approach to life makes her a wonderful person in her relationships. She is the kind of woman every husband would desire to live with because she has learnt the secret of sweet submission to her own husband. She does not see herself as superior or inferior to man, but as a suitable companion, sent by God to bring support and strength into His life. She does not demand appreciation for every good thing, she does she is very much content that her life is a source of blessing unto others. She knows her reward is with her God.

She does not get offended when she is overlooked or unappreciated; she is a woman of great character. She is peaceful and does not waste her time pondering over trivial matters; she is wise, and smart, considering the effect of her words and actions on people, before she relates to them. And this brings us to God's third statement about her "and One who trembleth at my word".

This attitude of the humble woman makes her the most blessed and fortunate because, to tremble at the word of God is to take a position of safety. A place of complete obedience to His will. To tremble at God's word, means to regard, respect, acknowledge, reverence and honor him. It means she places God in His rightful position of absolute authority in her life. Her faith in God is characterized by a life of obedience, faithfulness and trusts that is best expressed by Paul's word, "I know whom I have believed, and I am persuaded that He is able to keep that which I have committed unto Him against that day. And that "faithful is He that promised, who will also do it. The humble woman is completely assured of God's presence and love no matter what she may go through. She has learnt the secret of her relationship with God as that of a porter and His vessel. Therefore she is not discouraged when life's challenges confront her though she may not understand them all, she is assured of the fact that her father will surely cause it all to work out for her good.

In the end she knows she will emerge with the glory of refined gold that has passed through God's fire of purposeful trial. During her difficult times of testing she has only one desire, which is best expressed by John the Baptist "He must increase and I decrease" Therefore it's no wonder the abundant harvest of souls she reaps into God's Kingdom through her Christian testimony. For Jesus said, and I if I be lifted up, will draw all men unto my self." She lifts Jesus up in all her endeavors in life, and looks up to him, to bring to pass His divine purposes in and through her surrendered life and complete service.

The humble woman is a blessed woman indeed for upon her hungry heart the father pours out of His spirit without measure, which is evidenced by her abundant harvest of blessings.

CHAPTER TWENTY

THE PROUD WOMAN

To the proud woman the bible has this to say: "God resisteth the proud, but giveth grace unto the humble." James 4:6. Who then is this unfortunate woman who has lost so much favor with God, that He positions Himself to oppose her? Surely her's is not an enviable position to be in. For a place where God opposes, is a place of destruction. And so we will do well to discover enough about this woman, so that we can do ourselves the favor of avoiding her pathways.

The proud woman is one who does not see the need for God in her life, and whose estimation of herself, is one of superfluity and naughtiness. She does not have a sober attitude towards life, but like the narrow minded woman, believes very much in herself and therefore orders her life and that of those around her, based on her own judgment. Believe me when I say her life is a mess. She refuses counsel and correction of any kind, even if it comes in a gentle and loving manner. She does not trust or appreciate those who sincerely try to help her through good Christian counsel. She favors those who shower her with flatteries that drag her into her self-destructive ways. The proud woman has lost the pathway to life and peace, because the Bible says that "pride goeth before a fall." Her presumptuous attitude and actions land her in a lot of troubles. But instead of turning to God in true repentance and humility, she continues her lifestyle of rebellion unto her own damnation.

The proud woman is a foolish woman because she hates instruction, and pride is an attitude that drives away many blessings. A naturally beautiful, delicate and well-bred woman may live for a long time as a spinster or may not experience joy even as a married woman due to pride and arrogance. No man wants to live with a boss as a wife. Many marriages could have been saved if we had many more women learning the art of submission to God's word, even in the face of challenging marital circumstances. The Bible says: "Submitting yourselves therefore to God. Resist the devil, and he will flee from you." James 4:7. Again the Bible declares: "...And having in a readiness to revenge all disobedience, when your obedience is fulfilled. 2 Cor. 10:6. From a closer look at the above verses, it is no wonder that many Christian women have lost countless spiritual battles, because they lack commanding power over the enemy, due to their disobedience to God's word.

The Bible clearly states: If we submit to God first, then we can "resist the devil and he will flee from us." It also says, "When we learn to fulfill our obedience to God; we can then revenge every disobedience of evil forces that war against us." According to Phil: 2:5-11, Jesus victory and triumph over the devil, was because of His total submission to the Father's will. We learn from Jesus experience, that in spite of our human weakness, we can exercise spiritual authority and power over the enemy, if we learn to submit our lives to the Word of God and walk in true obedience to His will for our lives. "For whatsoever is born of God over cometh the World". 1 John 5:4.

It is therefore of little wonder that the proud and arrogant woman has so little fruits to boast of. Because of her lack of emotional balance and stability, she has lost many good relationships and opportunities. Like her sister the Cursed Woman, her feet is set on the path of defeat and shame. Oh what a pity! For her pride has blinded her eyes from the doors of opportunities, which God has placed before her. Yet through her ignorance and pride, she casts the blame on others. She does not see the need for correction in her own life.

The proud woman does not respect authority no matter what category it falls in. Be it in church, at home or in society, she is a source of public disgrace to her closest acquaintances. Through her tantrums, rage and loss of temper, she loses her self-control and picks a quarrel anywhere and anytime she gets offended, throwing her weight about not caring about the consequences. It is not surprising that the people that are close to her do not have the liberty to express themselves to her freely, for fear of offending her even slightly, creating an unpleasant situation.

In her home, she is either the boss or espiers to be. Everyone including her husband and children try their best to maintain peace by allowing her to have her way at all times. She is like a spoiled child, full of childishness and fussing. She delights in being in charge of her home atmosphere, but she does not consider the fact that she loses the trust and dependence of her family on her judgment, knowing how she reacts to challenging situations. It is a real pity, for any woman to be in such a situation in her own home.

The proud woman is a woman with a great deal of hidden fears and insecurities. She therefore abuses her position in the lives of the people who love her by imposing herself upon them, which gives her a little sense of achievement and helps her to cover up her emotional weakness. But all the same, her methods may vary depending on the situation or circumstance prevailing at that given time.

Sometime she uses noise, shouting and tantrums to dominate. And on other occasions, she uses the deceptive method of silent manipulation. Both methods make her look shameful and defeated. She is full of craftiness. For the proud woman, her only way of escape is to see herself as God sees her; a precious blessed, and unique individual whom he dearly loves. This realization will create in her the inner peace and assurance needed to make her appreciate herself so that she can learn to appreciate and respect others. Her breakthrough will come when she agrees with the open-minded woman that there's more to life than what she knows already. Once this happens, she will begin to respect and accept the good opinions and suggestions of others, for positive changes in her life and that of her loved ones.

It is a real pity when the proud woman raises children and produces husbands and wives for men and women who may not be able to handle the effects of her negative influence and control over their lives. For her children will ignorantly pick after her negative character, directly or indirectly. If God does not intervene in the homes and marriages of such badly raised children and give them the grace to submit to the counsel of God in humility their lives will end in sorrow and pain, not being able to handle the emotional challenges and responsibilities that go with marital life.

Let us elaborate on some of the attitudes of the proud woman which could be passed on to her children; for example; she lacks the simple courtesies of saying 'thank you' for favors done her, or I'm sorry when she wrongs someone, she does not have the ability to forgive and forget. She resorts to hateful and vengeful thoughts when offended and is never satisfied with any apologies rendered her. Until she gets even with her offender her heart will never be at rest. Because she is unforgiving, she does not know the sweet blessedness of God's forgiveness in her own life. And so her life is filled with guilt, anger, irritation and frustration.

Please if you know such a woman or live close to one, then I entreat you to pray for her and with patience and humility exercise a high level of self-control yourself and with the help of God, I believe you can be the tool God would use to turn her unhappy life around for His own glory. On the other hand, if you happen to see some of her characteristics in your own life as a woman, repent and turn to the Lord, for He is more than ready to help you restore Joy, Love and Peace into your life and that of your Loved ones. May the Lord help you experience this blessing, as you trust in His love. May the Holy Spirit release unto you His divine ability so that your life will begin to bear fruit and your Christian testimony and character will bring Glory unto God's Name. Amen.

FINAL WORDS OF ENCOURAGEMENT

Precious One, I believe it's been a very wonderful and sobering experience traveling together with the HOLY SPIRIT on this trip of Destiny. I hope you enjoyed His loving candidness as much as I did, and that you've also had the gracious opportunity of seeing your true image in the mirror of God's word. To be frank with you, I did see a lot of flaws in my own image as we sailed through some of the rough and unpleasant waters, but believe me, it was very refreshing and full of blessing.

I therefore encourage you to avail yourself to the HOLY SPIRIT, for he will release unto you strength for the needed change, and His love and refining fire will bring you to a place of peaceful rest and blessedness that will bring fulfillment to your life and glory to God. God loves you dearly, and in spite of all your short coming and failure, He patiently waits for you to take a bold step of faith, by accepting His Love, Forgiveness, Correction and Restoration, which can gradually transform you into the image of His Son. FOR THIS IS THE DESIRE OF THE FATHER, THAT WE BE COMFORMED TO THE IMAGE OF HIS DEAR SON.

Till we meet again at life's Harbor for another Trip of Destiny I say a big thank you and God Bless You.

It was nice coming your way.

SPECIAL PRAYER OF DEDICATION

Almighty Father, I thank you for this Trip of Destiny, and for the opportunity given me to look into the mirror of your word in my heart. Thank you for opening my eyes to see all the flaws in my image, and my need for change.

Father, I acknowledge my sins, rebellions and failures in the light of your word and I ask you to forgive me. Heal my heart of any pain, un-forgiveness and pride. Oh God, I ask you to empty me of my self and give me the grace to surrender my life completely to your will. Help me to walk in the SPIRIT and to crucify the flesh and it's canal desires. Please fill me with your divine attributes so that my character will be refined to reveal the beauty and blessed quality of a life that is totally yielded to your word, for your Glory and Praise. Father, make me a blessing to my Family, Church, Society and World. Thank you for hearing and answering my prayer in the name of Jesus Christ my Lord. Amen.

Precious Lady, God bless you for this humble Prayer, expect the results of your prayer; even an abundant and fruitful life. AMEN!

GATEWAY TO ABUNDANT LIFE

If you see your need for God, and have been convicted of your sins, and would love to have a personal relationship with Jesus Christ, I encourage you to reach out in faith and let us begin this blessed trip of Destiny into the Kingdom of God by confessing Jesus as Lord and accepting Him as Savior.

Let us begin with the Word of God; For all have sinned and come short of the glory of God. Rom **3:23**; For the wages of sin is death but the gift of God is eternal life through Jesus Christ our Lord. **Rom 6:23** ; But God Commendeth His Love toward us in that, while we were yet sinners, Christ died for us **Rom 5:8**; If we say that we have no sin, we deceive our selves and the truth is not in us. If we confess our sins, He is faithful and just to forgive us our sins and to cleanse us from all unrighteousness **I John 1:8-9** For God so loved the World that He gave His only begotten son that whosoever believeth in him should not perish but have everlasting life **John 3:16;** For God sent not His son into the world to condemn the world, but that the world through him might be saved .**John 3:17** Neither is there salvation in any other, for there is no other name under heaven given among men, whereby we must be saved **Acts 4:12;**. "If thou shalt confess with thy mouth the Lord Jesus, and shalt believe in thy heart that God hath raised him from the dead, thou shalt be saved. For with the heart, man believeth unto righteousness, and with the mouth confession is made unto salvation." **Rom. 10:9-10, 13**.

For the scripture saith whosoever believeth on him shall not be ashamed, for whosoever shall call upon the name of the Lord shall be saved. Precious one, God loves you and has made provision for your salvation you are not reading this book by chance, but by divine appointment, and today is the day of your salvation and restoration unto God, your Father. Please proceed with me in the Prayer of Salvation.

PRAYER OF SALVATION

Father, Abba Father, I thank you today for this timely opportunity given me, to put my life back on track. Father I know I am a sinner and I cannot save myself. I thank you for sending Jesus to die on the cross for my sins. I acknowledge my sins before you today, and ask for your forgiveness. Cleanse me in the blood of Jesus and save me from my sins in Jesus Name. LORD JESUS I confess you today as my Savior and accept you as my Lord, please come into my HEART today and makes me a new person in your most Blessed Name. **ALMIGHTY FATHER** I thank you for hearing my prayer and saving me in **JESUS NAME, AMEN.**

Thank You Jesus!! I Am Saved!!!

_____
Name

_____
Month   Day   Year   Time

_____
Signature

Printed in the United States
33694LVS00004B/406-438